What readers say about Harlequin Romances

"I feel as if I am in a different world every time I read a Harlequin."
A.T.,* Detroit, Michigan

"Harlequins have been my passport to the world. I have been many places without ever leaving my doorstep."
P.Z., Belvedere, Illinois

"I like Harlequin books because they tell so much about other countries."
N.G., Rouyn, Quebec

"Your books offer a world of knowledge about places and people."
L.J., New Orleans, Louisiana

*Names available on re

OTHER
Harlequin Romances
by NAN ASQUITH

699—THE HOUSE ON BRINDEN WATER
898—MY DREAM IS YOURS
1192—THE CERTAIN SPRING
1223—THE GARDEN OF PERSEPHONE
1261—WITH ALL MY HEART
1284—ONLY MY HEART TO GIVE
1476—BELIEVE IN TOMORROW
1734—THE GIRL FROM ROME
1753—TIME MAY CHANGE

Many of these titles are available at your local bookseller
or through the Harlequin Reader Service.

For a free catalogue listing all available Harlequin Romances,
send your name and address to:

HARLEQUIN READER SERVICE,
M.P.O. Box 707, Niagara Falls, N.Y. 14302
Canadian address: Stratford, Ontario, Canada N5A 6W2

or use order coupon at back of book.

Turn the Page

by

NAN ASQUITH

Harlequin Books

TORONTO • LONDON • NEW YORK • AMSTERDAM • SYDNEY

Original hardcover edition published in 1970
by Mills & Boon Limited

ISBN 0-373-01411-2

Harlequin edition published July 1970

Second printing April 1976
Third printing February 1977
Fourth printing March 1978

Printed in U.S.A.

CHAPTER 1

It was immense against the evening sky. A shadowy stone monster crouched above the town with a thousand jewelled eyes shining through the autumn dusk.

Munroe's—one of the biggest stores in the city. A huge, whirring storehouse of luxuries and necessities.

Cathie stared up at it in fascinated bewilderment. Great-Grandfather Munroe had built the business from a small shop in Corporation Street. Grandfather Munroe had carried it on. Cathie could remember him very well. Sharp blue eyes, trim, white imperial, stiff, old-fashioned high collar. After Grandfather—Father. After Father there was to be Tom, her brother.

She turned her head to Tom, who was standing close by her side. She and Tom were very alike. They had the same dark, curly hair, the same deep, black-lashed blue eyes, the same even features. Only Tom was tall and broad and Cathie was small and slim.

Tom felt her look. He swung round.

'Well, that's it, Cathie. That's the end.

Munroe's is finished—for us.'

Still Cathie couldn't believe it. She gestured helplessly towards the store.

'It seems impossible. I mean, there it is. Still going on. So huge and—and full. So busy. I can't believe we're bankrupt.'

Bankrupt! Munroe's had been the family business for over a hundred years, and yet today at the shareholders' meeting Cathie and Tom had learned that Munroe's was going into liquidation.

The reasons given were quite logical. At least, they had seemed so an hour or two ago, when they had been told all about profit and loss and S.E.T. and the squeeze and taxation and the huge overdraft waiting at the bank.

Mr. Carstairs, the family solicitor, had been there, and afterwards he had explained it all in more human terms.

'You see, Tom, your father was a sick man the last four years. He attended very little to the business personally. You'll forgive me, but he never, even when he was well, had the business head of his father, or of Robbie Munroe, your great-grandfather. His tastes lay in other directions. Things just went from bad to worse. He made no attempt to pull the business up, to move with the times. I think he was counting on you, Tom. He was waiting for you to finish at University and bring new blood and ideas into the business.'

'If only I'd known,' Tom said, 'but Father never told us. I felt out of touch with things.'

'Tom's right. Father never said or hinted that things weren't going well,' Cathie said to Mr. Carstairs.

'He wouldn't, Miss Catherine. He was far away from it all latterly.'

When it was over, it was Cathie who wanted to go home through the city.

'Let's walk, Tom. There's so much to talk and think about. And I'd like to walk past Munroe's.'

Now, outside its bright splendour, Cathie could have burst into tears.

'Poor Daddy! If—if he knew this had happened!'

Tom squeezed her arm.

'Maybe it was best he went when he did. It would have broken his heart.'

Cathie shook her head,

'His heart was broken before that, when Mother died.'

They were both silent a moment. Around and about them the shopping crowds thronged, the buses went grinding by. As they stood there, watching, the lights in Munroe's began to fade out one by one from the top floors.

'Closing time,' Tom said. 'Come on, let's get home, Cathie. You'll catch cold standing here.'

Cathie sighed.

'Closing time,' she echoed. 'The end of so much. The beginning of—what?'

She glanced up at Tom's firm brown chin as their steps quickened to a brisker pace.

'Tom, what will you do now?'

She saw a frown flicker over his set face.

'I'm not quite sure, Cathie. Thank goodness I don't have to worry about you. You'll be married soon and safely taken care of. Have you and Keith fixed a date for the wedding?'

'Not exactly,' Cathie said. 'We had thought of some time in November. Just a quiet wedding, Tom. Everything depends on finance. Have we any money left?'

Tom shrugged.

'I honestly couldn't say. We'll have to sell Willowmere, of course. But that won't help us much. The debts are so big. All I can hope for at most is a hundred—or two for you to live on until you're married.'

'But you?'

'Don't worry about me. I can always get along. Cathie, what would you say if I told you I—I'd like to emigrate?'

Cathie raised startled eyes to his.

'Go abroad, Tom?' For a moment she was

overwhelmed. Then she said, 'Do you mean you've something definite in view?'

'Not really definite. Only you remember Steve Gordon, the fellow who shared my rooms at University? He came and stayed with us one Christmas.'

'Yes, I remember.'

'We used to talk a lot about New Zealand where Steve came from. He was crazy to get back to it although he loved being in England. He called it a paradise. He used to say, 'I wish you could come back with me, Tom. That's the place for you. That's the life.' Tom smiled. 'When I used to tell him I was lined up for Munroe's, he would get quite fierce and say, "Shop-keeping! When you could be farming with me beyond Dunedin."

'And you think he'd still want you to go out to him?' Cathie asked.

'I think so. I had a letter from him a week or two ago. I thought of cabling him and suggesting it. But I wanted to ask you about it first.'

'It's not for me to say,' Cathie answered. 'It's your life, Tom.'

'Yes, but I'll be leaving you, Cath. And you're my responsibility. I must look after you. Though Keith Chandler's waiting to take over now, isn't he?'

'Of course. Send that cable, Tom. I want you

to. It's your great chance. There's nothing left for you here, now that Munroe's has gone. And you were never really keen on the store, were you? I know you did your best to hide it from Father, but your heart was never in it.'

Tom shook his head slowly. 'No, it wasn't really, but I didn't want to let Father down. I suppose that's why I never discussed the business much with him. In a way I was holding back from the idea.'

They were inside the iron gates of Willowmere now and walking up the wide drive. Home. For just a little while longer.

Already the big house had an air of emptiness and change. Already it seemed a stranger's house.

A short stout woman with rosy cheeks and grey hair cut in an uncompromising bob was watching for them.

'There you are! I was beginning to wonder about you. Miss Cathie, Mr. Chandler tele-phoned and he'll ring again in an hour's time.'

'Thank you, Maggie.' Maggie had been with the family since she was fifteen. Now she was the housekeeper and had helped run Willowmere for her father since Cathie's mother had died. Cathie felt a pang as she went slowly upstairs. They would have to break the news to Maggie and tell her what had happened and that she would not be able to stay with them.

Cathie looked round the big bedroom with its gold-painted furniture and deep-piled cream carpet. The rich apricot silk curtains were drawn against the autumn dusk. A small electric fire burned in the cream-tiled grate although the room had central heating. It was welcome in its luxury. Soon it would all be gone.

She braced herself. Material things were all very well, but they dwindled to unimportance beside the sad happenings of the last weeks. Her father dying, the old family business melting into nothingness before her eyes; Tom talking of going to the other end of the earth.

Maggie had brought the coffee in when the phone rang. It was Keith. His voice, warm and deep and reassuring, sounded as if he was in the room beside her.

'How are you, Cathie darling? How did the meeting go? I hope you haven't had a terribly grim day.'

Cathie hesitated. She longed to pour out all her troubles to him and ease the sense of bewildered despair by sharing it with him, but she couldn't, not over the telephone. It was too big a matter, too involved. Instead, she said, 'I'm afraid the news isn't very good.'

'Poor sweet, you sound tired and worried. Are you? Please don't be. Remember, I'm here and

I'm going to take care of you for good in a very little while.'

Cathie closed her eyes a moment, resting in the loving comfort of Keith's voice.

'It will be lovely to see you, Keith. Are you coming to fetch me?'

'Darling, that's why I'm calling. I'm held up here; car trouble. There isn't a train back until pretty late, but Mother is expecting you. Can you get up there on your own?'

Cathie felt a chill of disappointment.

'I think Tom is going out. He would run me up to your house in the car.'

'That's fine! With any luck, I'll be back in time to see you home, Cathie darling. There go the pips. Have a nice evening with Mother. Goodbye, sweet, and bless you.'

'Goodbye, Keith darling.'

The receiver clicked into place. She walked slowly back into the sitting-room to finish her coffee with Tom.

She sat in silence, stirring her cup.

It was odd how she dreaded the prospect of going on her own to Keith's house. She thought of Mrs. Chandler and the thin, beautiful face under the perfectly-groomed grey hair. She was like Keith in that her eyes were dark and lustrous, but her features were aquiline where Keith's were rugged, and her skin fine and pale. It was

odd, but Cathie had always been aware of a
faint hostility in Mrs. Chandler's manner.

It was only natural in a way. Her husband was
dead. Keith was her only child. She was intensely proud of him, intensely ambitious for him.
There was a law career for Keith, but mean-
time he was completing his studies before taking
his final degree.

Cathie shrugged, trying to feel philosophical
about it and hoping that time would win Mrs.
Chandler on to her side.

'Wake up!' Tom broke in cheerfully. 'You're
miles away. Will you be long getting ready? I
want to leave in about ten minutes.'

The Chandlers' house was on the outskirts of
Barrington, a fair distance away from the Munroes' home.

The house was small, but perfectly furnished.
Mrs. Chandler had exquisite taste in everything.
Nothing jarred the smooth harmony, nothing
ugly or out of place ever popped up in her home.

Tonight the delicate silver grey and violet of
Mrs. Chandler's drawing-room shone subdued
under the soft lighting. The bright fire and the
brilliance of enormous shaggy wine-coloured
chrysanthemums were the only splash of colour.
Mrs. Chandler rose from the damask-covered
chair by the fireplace.

'Catherine, my dear, come in. How cold your

hands are! Come along and sit by the fire. It's too wretched that Keith is delayed, but never mind, you and I can have a cosy little chat together on our own.'

The words were welcome enough and for a moment Cathie glowed into response. Then she was aware of Mrs. Chandler's cool sideways glance, and doubt flooded through her again.

She tried to make conversation, but it was difficult. There was always a feeling of awkwardness and constraint—as if Mrs. Chandler wasn't quite real. Yet she was Keith's mother. They were the same flesh and blood and Cathie loved Keith. It should surely have been easy to love his mother?

Mrs. Chandler leaned down and picked up a log with the fire tongs, placing it lightly but firmly on the back of the fire.

'You look pale, Catherine, and worried. I do hope you aren't worrying about anything.' Her voice dropped to a low sympathetic note. 'Of course, this has been a very sad time for you and your brother.'

It was an opening, and Cathie took it. She said steadily, 'I am rather worried, Mrs. Chandler. You see, Tom and I learned today, at the shareholders' meeting, that Munroe's is going into liquidation.'

She had caught Mrs. Chandler unprepared.

The still face broke up into startled dismay and for a moment the pale cheeks were flushed pink.

She said unevenly,

'Into liquidation! Are you sure?'

'Quite sure,' Cathie answered. She gave Mrs. Chandler a few brief details.

'I see.' Mrs. Chandler's voice was smoothly calm again. 'Does Keith know this?'

'Not yet. I didn't feel I could explain it to him over the telephone. He rang a little while ago.'

'No, of course not.' Mrs. Chandler stared thoughtfully into the glowing fire, and gave a little sigh. 'It is tragic for you my dear. Tell me, what are you and your brother going to do?'

'Tom has a chance to emigrate to New Zealand, to farm with a great friend of his from University.'

'And you, my dear?'

Cathie hesitated.

'I'm going to stay for a little while with some very old friends of ours, Dr. and Mrs. Nesbit, at Barnside. Then I may go to my aunt, Miss Watts, when she returns from London.'

She wanted to add, 'and then Keith and I hope to be married'. But somehow the words wouldn't come.

'Of course, you have something left of your own?' Mrs. Chandler inquired in a politely courteous voice. 'A little private income perhaps left to you by your father?'

Cathie shook her head. She felt a sudden coldness.

Mrs. Chandler's voice was bland and kind, like someone explaining a problem to a rather stupid child.

'My dear, I can see you don't understand the difference this makes. I am sure you haven't realised for a moment that this means the end of yours and Keith's hopes of marriage. At least, for the present.'

Cathie stared at her.

'You see,' Mrs. Chandler went on smoothly, 'Keith has no money of his own. He is not qualified as a solicitor yet. And I am afraid my means don't stretch to—well, to keeping both of you.'

Cathie felt her cheeks flush. She said quickly,

'I would never accept any help, Mrs. Chandler.'

'Of course not. I don't expect you to. You're a proud girl, Catherine, and a sensible one. I am sure you quite understand that, sympathetic as I am towards you, I must think of Keith and his career. He can't be handicapped at the beginning.' Mrs. Chandler shrugged her shoulders. 'If something had been salvaged out of the wreck and you had some money of your own, things might have been different. As it is—

well——'

Cathie wanted to cry out to plead—for what? She and Keith were young, they were in love. They were penniless. But they did not want Mrs. Chandler's charity.

She had a sudden awareness that Keith's mother had only tolerated her for her money, for the advantages that Munroe's would have given Keith. She looked at Mrs. Chandler, her chin tilting unconsciously, 'I hope—I hope to get a job of some kind.'

Mrs. Chandler smiled, 'My dear, what are you trained for? You're not a graduate. I seem to remember you telling me once that you left school at eighteen and stayed at home to look after your father and help round the house rather than try for a place at the University.'

'Yes, because my father was ill. He had a major operation that year. I felt my place was at home.'

'Of course,' Mrs. Chandler agreed smoothly, 'I respect your sense of duty, Catherine, but it has left you at a disadvantage in an increasingly competitive world.'

There was no answer to that. If only I'd been trained for something, Cathie thought desperately, but when Father began to be ill I never thought about it and I always thought that if Keith and I were to be married I should have a little money that would help him—at the beginning, anyway. She stood up with sudden abruptness.

'Mrs. Chandler, I don't think I shall wait for Keith. He may be very late home. If you'll excuse me, I'll go now. It's been rather a long day.'

'As you wish,' Mrs. Chandler said serenely. The soothing charm of her delightful room would never be disturbed by angry scenes or high words or arguments. Nothing would mar the even tenor of her life.

Cathie glanced round.

'I should like to leave a note for Keith, if I may.'

'Certainly.' Mrs. Chandler's eyes were suddenly wary as they met her glance. 'He will wonder why you have not waited for him.' She drew down the bureau lid. 'Here is notepaper and ink. Use it as you wish.'

'Thank you.'

Cathie wrote quickly and briefly. She said she was tired with the long, distressing day and gave a short account of Munroe's difficulties, then she handed it unsealed to Mrs. Chandler.

'I think Keith will understand.'

Her eyes searched for some warmth, some kindliness in the still face opposite her. Then she turned away. 'Goodbye, Mrs. Chandler.'

'Goodnight, Catherine. I am sorry to appear so disheartening over yours and Keith's plans, but I am sure when you think it over you will realise that I am right.'

Cathie made no reply, only hurried quickly away through the hall and out of the door into the autumn night.

She was lucky enough to catch a passing bus. She sat chilled and huddled in the seat, staring out at the black, blowy night beyond. It seemed at that moment as dark and uncertain as her own future.

When she reached home Tom was still out, but Maggie was waiting for her.

'About time, too,' she declared fiercely, 'with that white face on you! I'll run your bath and bring you a glass of warm milk to your bed.'

'Oh, Maggie!' The tears of weariness swam into Cathie's eyes. A doubt of her future seemed to fill her and she sat down on the edge of the bed.

'Maggie, Munroe's isn't ours any longer. All our money's gone. And Tom is going away to New Zealand.'

Maggie dropped the hot water bottle she had been on her way to fill.

'What are you saying, Miss Cathie? Surely you've taken leave of your senses?'

'No, I haven't. It's the end of everything for

us, Maggie.' Mrs. Chandler's proud, pale face seemed to float before her. She said heavily, 'Perhaps I shan't even be getting married.'

Maggie's worn, knotted fingers began unfastening her dress.

'Such nonsense,' she muttered. 'Into your bath now and then into your bed. I shall not be listening to such depressing talk tonight.'

She shook out Cathie's frock and hung it on a hanger, and as she turned away, she said over her shoulder, 'It's never the end of anything when a person's but twenty, Miss Cathie. Remember that. If there's to be changes, then changes will come. I've thought for some time, when your father was ailing, that maybe there might be some alterations. But where there's an ending, there's a beginning again. That's life. It's just a page turned over.'

Cathie paused at the bathroom door.

'Oh, Maggie, you make it sound so simple. But it isn't, you know. Still, I'll try to look at it your way.'

A hot bath warmed and soothed Cathie. She tumbled quickly into bed and there was kind Maggie with the hot milk and an aspirin at her side.

'Go to sleep, Miss Cathie, and don't worry. You've had worries enough the last few months. Goodnight now, and God bless you!'

CHAPTER 2

In the morning a cable came from Steve Gordon in answer to the one Tom had sent the day before.

It said, 'Imperative be here early October. Due in hospital end of month for operation on leg. Count on you to take over by then. Writing.'

Tom was full of it.

'What does he mean? I don't know a blind thing about farming. Take over!' he laughed. He looked both pleased and proud. 'Of course it's just to act for him, watch over the house and so on,' he explained to Cathie. He shot a look at her. 'You look awfully done up. I say, it isn't about my leaving, is it? And anyway, what about the wedding? You and Keith will have to push things on a bit, otherwise I won't be here to give you away.'

This was the moment to tell him, to explain that there might not be a wedding. But he looked so excited and happy for the first time in many weeks that she said, with a rather strained smile, 'That's not very easy, Tom. You know how much there is to arrange these days. We've nowhere to live. And you know, Keith isn't earning yet. There may be delays. But don't worry, I'll be all right with the Nesbits. I'm going to stay there.'

Tom's frown cleared.

'Steve's only given me a fortnight at this rate. I would like to go. It's bad luck on him having this trouble with his leg. I wonder if I can fix an air passage. One person can usually get a last-minute cancellation. Meanwhile, we've a terrific amount to do this end. I'm going right away to see Mr. Carstairs about fixing up the sale of the house and furniture, if you're agreeable.'

'Of course, Tom. Go ahead.'

What was it Maggie had said last night? Where there's an ending there's a beginning again. That was how it was for Tom. He had no sighs or regrets for yesterday.

And for herself? This should be the beginning of her life with Keith, but at the moment nothing was settled.

She sighed. She felt more unhappy and more alone in the particular moment than she had felt for a long time. She turned to cross the hall and the door bell rang.

It was Keith!

He stood there, tall, broad-shouldered, black-browed—a dark-haired Viking. He didn't speak.

He kicked the door to behind him and gathered her into his arms. They stood there in silence, arms about each other, not speaking, not kissing; just holding one another tightly.

Keith moved his cheek against her hair.

'Cathie.'

'Oh, Keith!' The whole world swung into focus again. The doubts and the fears and the shadows fled.

'I love you, Cathie.'

She blinked away the sudden tears.

'I love you.'

'Don't worry about a thing. We've got each other. Munroe's doesn't matter, money doesn't matter.'

Cathie moved back against the circle of his arm. Her fine brows puckered.

'Has your mother spoken to you, Keith?'

'She tried to talk, but I wasn't having any. I love you, Cathie, and we're going to be married.'

'But how?' Cathie protested. 'When we haven't any money.'

'I'm going to get a job,' Keith assured her. 'I'll chuck up law. There's plenty of things I can do.'

Cathie shook her head in quick dismay.

'No, Keith. No, I couldn't let you do that. It wouldn't be fair. Your mother has made sacrifices, she's done so much for you and you can't waste it all. You must stick to your studies and get your degree.'

'But it will be ages,' Keith cried. 'I've a lot to do yet.'

'We love each other,' Cathie said gently. 'So long as we believe in each other and have faith, everything will come out right. We'll be together one day.' She smiled. 'Darling, I'm the one who's going to get the job.'

Keith kissed the top of her head.

'Sweetie, what can you do? You're not trained for anything.'

'I can do something,' Cathie assured him. 'Oh, Keith, it won't be so long. You work hard at law and I'll work hard to keep myself and we'll meet every day and make plans and hope and dream, and one day the dream will come true.'

Keith hugged her to him.

'It will, won't it?'

'The only thing is, there's Tom. Please, dear, don't let him know how things are. He won't go if he knows we're not going to get married, and he'll miss his chance.'

She explained about Tom and his cable, how he had been so sure of Cathie's early marriage he had gone ahead with his own plans. She finished up rather wistfully, 'It isn't that your mother doesn't like me, is it, Keith? I feel that she's against me in some way.'

Keith frowned ruefully.

'It's nothing to do with you, darling. It's just that I'm Mother's ewe lamb, I'm afraid.'

Cathie reached up to kiss him.

'And mine,' she whispered.

Life was suddenly all comings and goings. Solicitors and house agents and auctioneers and prospective buyers. There were papers and documents to sign, Tom's things to pack up for shipment, to follow after he left by air.

Cathie's pearls and some bits of jewellery had been sold because she wanted to give Maggie something. Maggie had protested and tried to refuse the money.

'I can't take it, Miss Cathie. Why, all your things are going, and your nice new fur coat has gone back to the shop. This is a terrible time for us all.'

'Now, Maggie,' Cathie said firmly, 'you were the one to cheer me up the other night, so don't get all upset now.'

'I never thought to see you without a roof over your head,' Maggie wailed.

'But I have a roof over my head. I'm going to stay with Dr. and Mrs. Nesbit at Barnside.' She glanced at Tom's anxious face. 'For the time being. Until——' She had to steady her voice

to make it sound more certain than she felt
—'until I'm married.'

Maggie sighed.

'I'll never settle to living with my sister Bella.
Never. She was always that pernickety. I'll be
glad when you're wed, Miss Cathie, and I can
come back to you.'

Cathie patted her hand.

'Dear Maggie, I'll be glad, too. I can't wait
for the day.'

Saying goodbye to Tom was the very worst of
all. They had always been such close friends.

'Darling Tom, you will take care of yourself,'
Cathie cried. 'You will promise to look after
yourself in every way?'

'Of course I will, short of wrapping myself
up in cotton wool. Cath dear, be very happy
with Keith. He's a great fellow.' Tom hugged
her tight and then tilted her face up to him. 'You
are happy about everything, aren't you?'

'Of course, Tom, of course,' Cathie cried,
clutching his hand desperately. 'He's working
very hard. He has an examination before Christmas. That's why we seem at sixes and sevens.'
She clutched him suddenly, in a sudden onrush
of tears. 'Oh, Tom, the whistle's gone!'

'Goodbye—God bless you, Cathie.'

'Goodbye, goodbye!' Cathie called despairingly.

The train moved slowly out. To the last, Tom hung out of the carriage window, waving. Then the white speck of his face was a blur—was nothing.

He was gone.

Cathie couldn't attempt to fight the tears. She walked stumblingly down the long, crowded platform, her head bent, her handkerchief held unashamedly against her eyes.

That was that.

She felt terribly alone. If only Keith had been able to come to the station with her! But he was forced to be in court.

She tried to pull herself together. She smoothed back a hair and blew her nose, and as she did so the wet handkerchief fell out of her hand on to the platform.

Someone said, 'Excuse me, you dropped this.'

Cathie took the sodden, crumpled ball in one hand and met the sympathetically serious gaze of a young man, immensely tall, with red hair and eyes a brilliant vivid blue staring down at her in open sympathy.

He hesitated, seemed as if he would like to say something more. Then he gave a brief salute with his hand and turned away.

She passed through the barrier and out into the busy cobbled street leading from the station. A distant clock said eleven-thirty. She was meeting Keith for lunch, and at five Dr. Nesbit was calling at the hotel for her to drive out to Barnside.

There was a sort of solace in the crowd, in the morning bustle of the city. So many passing faces and people; so much rushing life. She thought that every one of them was the same as herself, wanting someone to love and to be loved by, wanting to be happy.

She had taken so much for granted. She had accepted money and love and a happy ending as the things that were bound to happen. But they didn't always, not unless you fought for them. For the right to possess such things.

'Where there's an ending, there's a beginning again,' Maggie had said. Somehow she couldn't forget those words. She would begin all over again, here in the city, working and hoping and loving, so that one day she and Keith would be together always.

The white façade of Stirling's—Stirling's which had always been such a rival to Munroe's —towered above the buildings at the end of the street. A row of flags fluttered from the roof, the bright autumn sunshine glinting on the many windows.

Cathie walked slowly towards it as if drawn by an invisible hand, and as she came up to the huge plate-glass window ahead of her she saw in it a white square of card.

'Wanted, Indoor staff of all kinds. Previous experience not essential.—Apply the Staff Manager.'

It was a sort of sign—an omen. She stared at it, reading again the words 'Previous experience not essential' and the next minute she had put her hand on the door and pushed it open.

The Staff Manager's office was on the fourth floor. A narrow corridor led from the back staircase towards a glass-panelled door marked 'Staff Manager, Private'.

A thin, sandy-haired woman, waiting in the corridor, smiled shyly at Cathie and she gave a tentative smile in return.

The door marked 'Private' opened and a plump, brown-haired girl came out.

'Who's next?'

The little woman stepped forward in a brisk movement like a hop.

'I'm next, miss.' She smiled over her shoulder at Cathie. 'Don't suppose I'll be very long.'

Cathie smiled back without answering.

Through the open doorway she could see a small, square room with a desk and filing cabinet in it. In the far wall was another door marked 'Private' again.

'Will you go right through,' the brown-haired girl said. 'Mr. Childers is waiting.' She turned to Cathie. 'Would you like to wait in my office? There's a spare chair there and,' she smiled, 'you're the only one left now.'

Cathie followed her into the office and sat down on a small, hard chair. She looked about her and met friendly brown eyes regarding her across the desk.

'Have we—have I met you before somewhere before?' the girl asked.

Cathie shook her head.

'I don't think so.'

'Your face looks sort of familiar. What sort of a job are you after?'

Cathie hesitated.

'I—don't really know. You see, I haven't had any previous experience and I'm not trained for anything. Just seeing the notice made me think I might—there might be a chance. I do need a job.'

'Of course,' the other said cheerfully. 'Don't worry about previous experience. We're taking on quite a lot of extra staff. You'll be all right. Have you any particular fancy? You don't type, I suppose?'

'No,' Cathie said. She added: 'I was rather keen on art at school, sketching and painting, but that's not much use here.' She straightened her shoulders and sat up a little straighter. 'I just want a job.'

The girl smiled.

'Fine.' She slid some paper in her typewriter and began to tap busily away.

After a time the little woman reappeared. She gave Cathie a cheerful grin. 'I've been lucky, luv. Hope you're lucky too.'

'Thank you,' Cathie whispered as she stood up and moved towards Mr. Childers' office.

Mr. Childers was short and dark and quiet. He asked Cathie a lot of questions and doodled on a pad in front of him. He raised a crooked eyebrow at the particulars of her expensive education but made no remark. Then he told her that subject to a medical examination in the Welfare Department she was free to start whenever she could do so.

'Next Monday?' Cathie asked. He nodded agreement.

'Check in here first. I'll see you then. Good morning, Miss—er—Munroe.'

That was that.

Cathie seemed to float out of his office.

It had happened! She had got a job. Some of the heartache of Tom's departure lifted. She felt happier and a little excited and apprehensive all in one breath. She longed to tell Keith immediately. She was to be in the perfumery department, the very nicest sort of department to be in. The sort of department she would have chosen if she had thought long enough about it. It was all such a piece of good luck.

She didn't know that it was her soft voice, the clear pallor of her complexion, her soft, dark prettiness, that had influenced Mr. Childers in his selection. She was just the type of girl they were after for the cosmetic counter. Mr. Childers had decided that her dark hair and deep blue eyes would look perfect above the tailored, ice-blue coat overalls worn by the perfumery girls. It helped to outweigh the fact of her inexperience.

Brown Eyes was smiling at her.

'Got what you want?'

Cathie came down to earth.

'Oh, yes. Yes, thank you. I'm to start in the perfumery on Monday.' She frowned. 'That is, I have to pass a medical examination first.'

The girl laughed.

'Just routine, so we won't run riot with measles, rabies or bubonic plague. I should go along there now if I were you. Welfare's in the basement.' She stood up. 'Look, I'm going down that way now. I'll take you.' She closed one of the desk drawers. 'My name is Sheila Cochrane. What's yours?'

'Cathie Munroe.'

'Munroe? Any relation of THE Munroes?'

Cathie wavered.

'Just—just slightly.'

Sheila grinned.

'Bet you're a poor relation, like I am. Ever heard of Sir Oswald Cochrane, the Cornflake King?' Her throaty laugh was infectious. 'He's the cousin of a cousin of a cousin of mine!' She pulled open the door. 'Come on, I'll show you the way.'

There were tantalising glimpses of various departments as they hurried down the stairs. Neat units of furniture; sleek television sets, spring interior mattresses and padded divan headboards on the fourth floor. Soft furnishings on the third was a flower garden of fabric and colour and on the second there were shining pelts of furs and a blur of tweed coats. They had reached the first floor where shimmering bales of materials made rainbow sweeps on counter and stand. Someone waited at the bend of the stairs for them to pass—a tall, red-headed young man.

Sheila said warmly, 'Hello there.' She turned to Cathie. 'This is Alec Hamilton, our genius from advertising. Alec, meet Miss Catherine Munroe, who starts here on Monday.'

Cathie stared up into the two vivid, intensely blue eyes that she had encountered at the railway station earlier that morning.

His look was bright and interested. It warmed into remembered sympathy as if he searched for some sign of those earlier tears and the distress that had been so clear on her face when she said goodbye to Tom.

'Hello.' He smiled gently. 'This is nice.'

He looked so friendly and so kind that Cathie smiled back in impulsive liking.

'Hello,' she answered shyly.

Sheila was watching them in a puzzled sort of way. She said, 'It's Cathie's first job. She's starting in perfumery.'

Alec Hamilton lifted a sandy eyebrow.

'You're lucky. I understand perfumery is one of those departments that you work up to, as a rule.' He grinned down at Cathie. 'I guess I'm going to take an awful lot of interest in lipsticks from now on!'

Cathie had to smile again.

'I expect I shall make a lot of mistakes at first.'

Alec was still gazing at her.

'Well, I'll be seeing you.' He gave Sheila a casual glance. 'Cheer-oh, Sheila. Goodbye, Miss Munroe.'

'Goodbye.'

Sheila looked sideways at Cathie as they went on down the stairs.

'Alec's a lot of fun. Everybody likes him.'

Cathie could believe that. There was something very likeable and alive about him.

They had reached the crowded basement. Sheila led the way past stacks of shiny aluminium saucepans, past galvanised iron dust bins and brightly-painted kitchen cabinets. At one end of the floor a cream door said, 'Welfare. Staff Only.'

Sheila nodded towards it.

'Go right through. One of the girls will look after you.' She gave Cathie her warm smile. 'If I don't see you again I'll watch out for you on Monday. Good luck.'

'Thank you,' Cathie said, 'Thank you very much, Sheila. Goodbye.'

CHAPTER 3

KEITH was waiting for her at the Connaught. It was a small restaurant where they could linger and talk undisturbed and was a favourite meeting place.

He stood up as Cathie approached the table, so tall, so handsome, that her heart warmed with the sudden uprush of love that Keith's presence always called up in her.

'Darling, come and sit here.' His hand closed over her own on the tablecloth. 'How are you, Cathie? Was it very awful seeing Tom go?'

Cathie nodded.

'It was rather. Like a bit of me being sliced away. That dreadful forlorn feeling that it wasn't just Tom going but a part of our lives which will never return."

'I know.' He squeezed her fingers tightly. 'But Tom will love it. He'll be happy and I know he'll make good.'

'Yes, I feel that. This is his chance.' The shadow on Cathie's face lifted. 'Oh, Keith, I've got some more cheerful news. I have a job!'

Keith stared at her, his dark eyes widening.

'Gosh, Cathie, that's quick work. Where? Tell me all about it.'

'It's at Stirling's.' Cathie broke off as the waitress came for Keith's order. After he had given it and the waitress had bustled away she said breathlessly, 'I'm going to start in the perfumery department on Monday. Oh, Keith, it is a beginning, isn't it? I shall be able to keep myself and we'll be able to get married quite soon.'

Keith was more cautious.

'Will you like it, Cathie? It will be hard work, long hours. You don't think something in the line of a receptionist's job would have suited you better?'

'Oh, no, Keith. I like shops. They're sort of self-contained worlds of their own. So many people, all with something to do that seems important to them.' Her dark blue eyes sparkled. 'I believe there's a streak of Grandfather Munroe in me. I felt absolutely at home there today and really I'm rather thrilled about it.'

Keith was watching her vivid face in loving amusement.

'So long as you're happy, darling. Anyhow, I think a job's a good idea quite apart from the financial side. It will help to ease your first break with Tom and with your old life.'

'I love you so very much,' Cathie said softly.

Because that was Keith all over. Understanding and sweet. Sympathetic. Harmony flowed between them, a warm bright current of trust and affection.

Cathie told him about Sheila. She mentioned Alec Hamilton too, adding, 'I think Sheila likes him rather. The way she spoke about him was nice. And I saw her looking at him.'

'You old matchmaker!' Keith teased. 'You're always thinking people are in love with one another. And how do people look that way?' He stared intently at her. 'Can you tell how I feel, Cathie, when I look at you like this?'

Cathie looked demure.

'I'm not sure. You'd have to gaze at me a lot more languishingly than that for me to be able to tell.'

'With Mr. Meredith, of Meredith, Meredith & Potts, watching me across the room for all he's worth? I will not!'

His voice changed and sobered.

'What time do you go out to Barnside?'

'Dr Nesbit is calling for me at five. I'm looking forward to my visit. They're both such dears, like sort of second parents in a way.'

Keith frowned.

'If Mother had felt a bit differently about things you could have come to stay with us.'

'Never mind,' Cathie consoled. 'I do understand. She'll change her mind, I'm sure. It's just that finding out I'm not going to have any money, not be any help at all to you, Keith, only a hindrance, has been a shock to her. It hurts in a way to feel that your mother only put up with me as a daughter in-law-to-be because I was expected to have a thousand a year of my own.'

Keith reached for her hand again.

'What does that matter, sweetheart? We love each other and money doesn't enter into it. I won't always be grinding away at these studies. One day I'll be independent and we'll be married.'

'I'm independent now,' Cathie assured him. 'At least, I will be after Monday, won't I? So we shan't have to wait awfully long to get married.' Her eyes closed. 'I can see it all. Two rooms at the top of one of those tall grey houses in Henshawe Terrace. The ones with the view of the river. We'll furnish them with some antiques and a few bits of my own I put in store. You can distemper the walls and I'll paint all the windowsills and skirting-boards and we'll both stain the floors starting at each end and meeting in the middle.'

She opened her eyes as Keith laughed. He said, 'Darling, you make it sound so real.'

'It will be,' Cathie assured him.

He glanced at his wrist watch. 'Curse it! Two

o'clock already. I'll have to go, Cathie.'

'But you're coming out to Barnside on Sunday for lunch and tea,' Cathie reminded him as they walked towards the swing door. 'Mrs. Nesbit particularly asked you.'

'Yes, I'll manage to survive somehow until Sunday, when I'll be with my Cathie.'

They stood in the street staring at one another.

'Darling.'

'Darling.'

It was a language all their own. One brief word and all their love and longing and hopes and dreams behind it.

A decorous kiss amidst the lunch-hour throng.

'Until Sunday, sweet.'

'Goodbye, Keith dear.'

A slow walk back to the private hotel where she and Tom had spent the last hurried days. Her packing was all but done. Heaviness returned to her heart. Where was Tom now? Was he thinking about her? Was he, too, sad for all the changes in their lives? Or had he turned the page without regret, already planning new adventures and fresh happenings?

She made an effort to forget—had a wash and powdered her face, tucked away some last-minute things in a suitcase, then went down into the lounge, where she wrote a letter or two and waited for Dr. Nesbit, to come and collect her.

It was a little after five when he arrived. Cathie had known him all her life, he and his wife had been close friends of her father. He was a big burly man with a high colour and heavy jowl, rather like a kindly St. Bernard.

'Well, Cathie?' His deep-set brown eyes twinkled down at her from under lowering eyebrows. 'I see you're all ready and waiting for me like the good girl you are.' His two broad hands clasped her own small one. 'Did Tom get away all right?' he asked gently.

'Yes, Uncle Robert.' He was no relation, but Cathie couldn't remember when she hadn't called him 'uncle'.

'I can see the grieving look in your eyes, Cathie, but remember it's a fine chance he's taking. What I wouldn't give for the old days when I was a ship's doctor on the Australian run.' He gave a gusty sigh. 'Tom will never want to come back to the fogs of Barrington again.' He caught sight of Cathie's face, and added hastily, 'Well, I mean not for a while. Where's your luggage, Cathie? We'll get going, shall we?'

Her cases were stowed away and Dr. Nesbit clambered into his ancient creaking car and started the engine up.

He turned to Cathie when they had left the cobbled streets of Barrington behind them.

'How is Keith? Your Aunt Jean said we're to

expect him out to see us on Sunday.'

'Yes, thank you very much for asking him. I told Keith about it today when we met for lunch. Oh, Uncle Robert, what do you think? I've got a job!'

Dr. Nesbit's tufty grey eyebrows shot up questioningly.

'A job?'

'At Stirling's.' Cathie related her morning's experiences to the doctor.

An enormous hand in a shabby leather gauntlet reached out to pat her arm.

'You're a brave girl. I wish you good luck. When do you start?'

Cathie looked at him hesitatingly.

'On Monday, Uncle Robert. So I won't be having a very long visit with you, will I? But I wondered if I could leave some of my luggage at Barnside.'

'And what's the hurry away?' Dr. Nesbit demanded fiercely. 'What's to prevent you staying with your Aunt Jean and me and going on the train to Barrington each morning? It's but five miles out of the town.'

Cathies face lit up.

'May I? It seemed rather cheek to think of it —out all day like a lodger. I thought I'd have to find digs or something.'

'You'll be our lodger,' Dr. Nesbit declared. He

beamed down at her. 'Though I was hoping for a little more of your company on my calls than I'll be having, Cathie.'

She smiled back, remembering the days when as a small girl the greatest joy of her life was to go out with the doctor and 'his little black bag' on some of his rounds; sitting patiently in the car with a picture book or being invited into some friendly house to be given a biscuit or a sweet while the doctor made a call.

Barnside was a small village on the outskirts of Barrington. It was quite unspoilt, although so near the town. A shallow stream babbled through it; a grey stone bridge, a cluster of grey stone houses and the grey spire of a church jostled along one side—on the other, trees and hedges climbed the gently rising hill.

The doctor's house was flush on to the main street, a square, double-fronted, friendly dwelling with a green-painted surgery door at one end. Two shallow steps led up to a handsome oak door lit with gleaming brass knocker and plate.

Mrs. Nesbit was on the threshold to greet Cathie, pulling her into a quick and loving embrace. She was a short, plump little woman with auburn hair fading into grey and bright periwinkle-blue eyes.

'My dear lassie! Come along in. Tea's ready

for you both. Robbie, Mrs. Dempster telephoned but it's not urgent, despite what she says. You're not to go out until you've had a bite to eat.'

Dr. Nesbit was reading the written message.

'I'll thank you to let me decide about my patients, Jean.' But his jolly twinkle belied the gruff words.

Tea was a white expanse of cloth beneath a rosy shaded light; shining silver and gilt-edged flowered china and tempting scones and cakes.

There was much to tell and talk about. They spoke of Tom. There were happy reminiscences and a few sighs, and brisk discussions of the future. Of Cathie's new job and her plans for marriage.

Later that evening, as she said goodnight to Dr. and Mrs. Nesbit, Cathie thought how astonishing it was that, although this was the day Tom had left to go far away, she felt happier and more at peace than she had done for a long time.

During the next few weeks Cathie discovered something else.

In her new life she seemed a different person, as if an unknown part of her came into being and thought and talked and acted through new eyes. Some part of the old Cathie had gone for ever and in the novel atmosphere of store life another Cathie saw things all afresh.

Sometimes she wondered which was real. The Catherine Munroe who had driven her own car; worn beautiful clothes; gone to dinners and dances; been the companion of her father in his invalid life. Or this Cathie, the one-of-a-crowd who surged into the back entrance of Stirling's each morning under the vigilant eye of Kenny, ancient doorman, hastening to clock-in, leaving coat and hat in the crowded cloakroom, pouring along the shrouded aisles towards the blue and gold façade of the perfumery.

At first she had felt lost and bewildered among it all. Everybody seemed engrossed or in a hurry, intent upon their own lives. Then, out of a sea of faces, there was Sheila, plump and smiling and brown-eyed, like a friendly robin. The other assistants in the perfumery ceased to be staring alien faces and turned into Peggy and Sandra and Val. And she herself became Cathie, one of them.

Each day she lunched in the immense staff canteen. She and Sheila had managed to coincide their lunch-hour break and established themselves at the same table. Alec Hamilton, she discovered later, ate in the superior glory of the sales manager's room, owing to the fact that he was 'administrative' staff.

Stirling's remained open all day Saturday and closed half-day on Thursdays. In some ways this was satisfactory, in others it was not. By mid-week Thursday loomed ahead as a welcome break. On the other hand, working all day Saturday made Cathie's week-end very short, the more so as Keith was always free on Saturday afternoons. They had been meeting for lunch on Thursdays so far, but always Keith had to return to work, leaving Cathie with the empty afternoon ahead.

Now it was Cathie's third Thursday at Stirling's, and at the last minute Keith had had to cancel their lunch arrangement.

Cathie wondered what to do with herself as she came out into the soft still air of the autumn day. She stood a moment on the pavement, glad of its cool freshness. Val went hurrying by on the arm of Johnny Grant from carpets and linoleums, calling, 'Cheerio, Cathie, have a nice afternoon.' Sheila had gone already.

She crossed the road and walked towards one of the cafés. She had to eat somewhere—even alone! She half-decided to catch a tram later and go up to Highton, the little suburb where Maggie was living with her sister. She had meant to visit Maggie long before now.

The Owl Café was halfway down Brownlow Street, its red brick front overshadowed by the cream stucco and green-painted window boxes of the Grand Central Hotel. As Cathie drew level a taxi halted outside the hotel, a slim grey-haired woman stepped out and handed the driver some coins, then turned towards the swing doors.

A cool, gracious voice said:

"Why, Catherine, my dear, how nice! It seems such a long time since I saw you. How are you, and where are you off to?'

A smoothly-gloved hand took her own, and Cathie found herself looking up into Mrs. Chandler's appraising dark eyes.

'How do you do, Mrs. Chandler? I—this is my free afternoon, Thursday, you know. I expect Keith told you I work at Sterling's now.'

'But of course! How very enterprising of you.' Mrs. Chandler put a hand on her arm. 'I do hope you haven't had your lunch. I was just going in here. Do have some with me.'

Cathie hesitated.

'I can see you haven't. I won't take "No," Catherine, so come along with me.'

They went through the doorway and along the thickly-carpeted corridor and into the warmth and light of the restaurant. An attentive waiter led them to a corner table where Mrs. Chandler slid back the soft furs from her shoulders and studied the menu.

When she had given the order she smiled across at Cathie.

'This is very nice. And you look well, considering. There is so little fresh air in those big stores, isn't there? And where are you living now? I'm sure Keith told me, but I have forgotten.'

'With Dr. Nesbit, out at Barnside. I wonder if you know him?'

'Oh, yes. An elderly doctor, isn't he—a little old-fashioned, of course, but still—country people are so antagonistic towards anything new. I expect he suits his practice very well.'

The waiter brought soup, and there was silence between them for a moment or two. Then Mrs. Chandler said, 'So you work on Saturday. Such a pity! I don't suppose you and Keith manage to see very much of each other except on Sundays?'

'We meet in the evenings sometimes,' Cathie answered, 'when he isn't studying. And sometimes on Thursdays for lunch. As a matter of fact,' she added, 'I was meeting him today, but he couldn't come at the last minute.'

Mrs. Chandler smiled slowly. She helped herself to some vegetables. 'I don't suppose Keith has had time to tell you this yet, my dear, but this has been a most important week for him. He has been given the opportunity to join Seymour & Watkins just as soon as he is through his examinations. Mr. Seymour was a great friend of my husband's and he has offered Keith this chance. I don't need to tell you how proud and happy I am, how relieved. Of course, Seymour & Watkins is quite the most important legal firm in the city. I expect you know that.'

Cathie's eyes were like stars.

'But—but how wonderful, Mrs. Chandler! Oh, I am so glad. For your sake as well as Keith's. He does deserve this chance. He's been working so hard. It will be a wonderful opportunity for him.'

Mrs. Chandler's deep-set eyes stared directly at her.

'Why, that is exactly what Mr. Seymour said to me. He has always thought the world of Keith.' She sighed. 'I think because he has no son of his own. It is as if he looks upon Keith as the one he might have had.' She glanced at Cathie. 'Black or white coffee, my dear?'

She poured out some coffee and handed the cup to Cathie.

'Of course, he has a daughter, Melanie. Quite one of the most beautiful girls I have ever seen. She and Keith have always been great friends.' She arched an eyebrow at Cathie. 'In fact, my dear, if Keith hadn't met you when Melanie was away in Paris studying at the Sorbonne I really think something would have come of their great interest in one another.'

Cathie felt suddenly drained of her first happiness and hope.

She watched Mrs. Chandler settling her stone martens about her shoulders again.

'I have so enjoyed our lunch together and our little talk,' the older woman went on. 'So nice to see you again, Catherine. You must come up to dinner one evening. Did I tell you Melanie Seymour was home from Paris? I want to give a little party for her.'

'That will be lovely,' Cathie answered. 'Thank you very much, Mrs. Chandler.'

'Take care of yourself. You do look rather pale, my dear. Goodbye for the present. You'll be hearing all about everything from Keith, I'm sure.'

Cathie stood staring after the slim, upright figure as she walked lightly and firmly across the road. She wondered why her heart felt suddenly heavy, full of a sort of doubt and apprehension. When she had just heard this wonderful news! Because surely this chance for Keith meant another step along the road towards their future?

The phrase echoed in her mind like a bell.

'Quite one of the most beautiful girls I have ever seen.'

She turned up the road towards the bus stop. Why should that trouble her? Didn't she know that it was herself Keith loved?

CHAPTER 4

MAGGIE was delighted to see Cathie. Her round rosy face lit up into a shining beacon of happiness.

'Oh, Miss Cathie, come in. There isn't a day I don't think about you and Master Tom.'

She led the way along a narrow passage. 'Will you excuse the kitchen?' she said apologetically, flicking a duster over the old-fashioned rocking chair. 'We've a big fire in here.'

Cathie smiled, glancing around at the spotless cosy room.

Maggie stood opposite to her, staring with anxious eyes.

'So you're working in a shop.' She moved the kettle to the centre of the stove, and sat down heavily in a tall, wooden chair. 'Tell me all about youself, Miss Cathie. And how is Mr. Keith? And when will the wedding be?'

'I don't know where to begin,' Cathie said. 'The shop's fun, Maggie. I've made a very nice friend, a girl named Sheila Cochrane. I'm busy all day, and when you're busy you haven't time to be miserable, have you? Mr. Keith is very well. I had lunch with his mother today, and he's going into partnership with the firm of Seymour & Watkins just as soon as he's through his final exam.'

'That's real good news,' Maggie agreed. 'Likely you'll be able to settle your plans soon.' The corner of her mouth turned primly down. 'Mrs. Chandler's a very grand lady, I'm sure,' she added.

Cathie's smile deepened, but she made no comment.

'How are you, Maggie? And your sister, is she well?'

'Oh, Bella's fine! She's away down at her daughter's. A good thing, too. I'm not sorry to have you to myself. Bella and me, we rub along pretty fair, but it's her home, not mine.' She sighed gustily. 'I'm going out to work three mornings a week, to oblige an invalid lady.'

She stood up and began to lay the table. 'You'll stay to take a cup of tea with me, Miss Cathie?'

'It's very kind of you, Maggie. Thank you.'

'And how's the doctor?' Maggie inquired, pouring out a strong brew into pretty flowered tea cups.

Cathie frowned.

'I don't think he's too well. He gets so tired, and he has far too much to do. It's a huge practice. There's such long distances to cover. He ought to have some help. But he won't listen to Aunt Jean and me, he just laughs and says he can manage.'

'He's a good man,' Maggie remarked. 'Will you have some spice bun, Miss Cathie? It's your favourite.'

Bella had not returned before Cathie rose to go. She said goodbye to Maggie and sent a message to her sister and gave warm thanks for the cosy pleasant tea by the fireside.

'It's been grand to see you,' said Maggie, clasping her hand at the door. 'Give my love to Master Tom when you write, and I'll be making the effort myself for him, never fear.'

'Don't forget to call in at Stirling's when you're in the town,' Cathie said. 'I'm on the ground floor, in the perfumery. Goodbye, Maggie.'

She turned at the end of the little street, and waved back.

The bus rocked and rolled like a crazy sort of ship riding the hills down into Barrington. She jumped off at the station, and walked across the cobbled yard into its dusky, echoing gloom. The Barnside train didn't leave for half an hour. The brightly-lit bookstall beckoned, and she made her way through a maze of people towards it.

She glanced through the cheerful display of

magazines and books and picked up a novel with a rather enticing cover.

'Recommended for strong stomachs only,' a voice said over her shoulder. 'It contains at least four corpses, and several buckets of blood.'

She turned to meet Alec Hamilton's laughing eyes.

'Hello,' she smiled

'We're fated to meet on stations,' he said. 'Are you coming or going?'

Cathie gave him a puzzled smile.

'What do you mean?'

'Are you coming into Barrington for the evening, or leaving it?'

'Leaving it,' Cathie answered. 'I'm waiting for the Barnside train.'

Alec lifted an eyebrow towards the station clock.

'It doesn't go for half an hour. That means you've time to have tea with me.'

'I've just had some tea,' Cathie protested.

He cupped her elbow with one hand.

'There's no limit to tea drinking. Over here. On our right.'

'But really——' Cathie began.

'Please,' Alec said, his voice suddenly serious. 'I'd like you to, very much.'

They found a quiet corner table in the station tea room.

Alec was smiling again.

'What have you been doing on your afternoon off?'

'I had lunch at the Grand Central and then went up to Highton to see a very old friend.'

'Where you had tea?' Alec asked.

'Where I had tea,' Cathie echoed smilingly.

'And where are you off to now?'

'I'm going home to Barnside.'

'Is that where you live?' he asked.

'It's where I'm staying,' Cathie answered. She became aware of Alec's intent stare, and broke off.

Alec nodded.

'I know, I'm being terribly rude, asking so many questions, being so curious. But I honestly want to know. I want to know everything about you. I have done from the start.'

Cathie felt herself colouring.

'It can't interest you.'

'But it does,' Alec insisted. 'You see, you interest me, Cathie.'

It was the first time he had used her christian name. Cathie was silent. She didn't know quite what to say, how to answer the sudden intimacy of Alec Hamilton's approach. Was he trying to do a line with her? Yet under his smile and his teasing ways she sensed a seriousness.

'Where is your real home?' Alec went on. 'I

mean—you say you're only staying at Barnside. Do you live in Barrington?'

Cathie met his look.

'I haven't any real home at present. My father died two months ago, and I'm staying with some friends of the family—until I get married.'

Alec's expression didn't change, but suddenly it was emptied of light.

'Married?' he said. He glanced down at Cathie's slim ringless fingers. 'But I'd no idea— d'you mean—you're engaged?'

'Unofficially,' Cathie said in a low voice. She glanced away from Alec, reaching out for his emptied cup and pouring fresh tea into it.

'I see,' Alec said quietly. He added, 'Sorry, I sounded rather an ass just now. Only—I did happen to mean it, Cathie, and it still stands. Everything about you does interest me.' He met her eyes. 'When—when are you planning to be married?'

Cathie hesitated.

'I don't know. You see, Keith, my fiancé, has still to get his degree in law. We haven't any money or anything. I've got this job at Stirling's and that's going to help.' Her face brightened. 'But I've heard today that there's the chance of a partnership for him with one of the best firms in Barrington.'

'Was it Keith you had lunch with?'

Cathie shook her head.

'With his mother. I usually do see Keith on Thursdays, but he couldn't manage today.'

Alec went on staring at her.

'You'll think I'm awfully rude, Cathie, but were you connected with the Munroes who've just gone bust?'

'James Munroe was my father,' Cathie answered slowly.

Alec nodded.

'I thought so. All along I've known there was something different about you. Forgive me, it isn't just curiosity. Ever since I saw you that first day here—you won't remember, maybe, but I couldn't forget the look in your eyes, your forlornness.'

'I do remember,' Cathie said quietly.

His face lit up.

'Do you? Look, Cathie, can't we be friends? Real friends, I mean. I hate to think because— because you're hitched up to someone else that's the end of everything. Before we've even begun. After all, a fellow and a girl can be friends. Platonic and all that, I mean.'

'Can they?' Cathie asked wistfully. There was something so warm and alive about Alec, so gay and impulsive. It would be nice to have a friend like him.

'Of course, what's his name—Keith, is it—he

won't mind, will he? I mean, I expect he knows girls you don't know.'

Cathie thought about Melanie Seymour. Did she begrudge Keith his long-standing friendship with her?

She said doubtfully, 'I don't see why we shouldn't be friends.'

'Alec,' he prompted.

'Alec.'

'Good.' Alec looked at his wrist watch. 'You've missed your train. Does it matter drastically? Personally, I'm delighted. We can go on talking for nearly another hour.'

Cathie sat up in startled dismay.

'Alec! No!'

'Yes. Look, have another cake. One of these fierce pink things. And tell me how you like working at Stirlings.'

Somehow you couldn't be cross with Alec. Cathie smiled.

'I must catch the six-five,' she insisted.

Alec gestured with his finger across his throat. 'On my oath.'

It was easy to talk to him. Cathie found herself telling Alec many things. About Tom going to New Zealand. About Maggie. Even a little about Keith, and Mrs. Chandler's disapproval of their love for one another. And in the telling there was a certain relief; a sense of warm interest and understanding opened up to her—there for the taking.

When they had finished tea they walked slowly across to where Cathie's train came in.

Alec waited to see her off.

'Thank you for having tea with me,' he said. 'This has been my lucky Thursday. See you to-morrow, Cathie. I'll be hovering around the perfumery. We're going to feature the department in the newspapers next week, so you'll be able to give me some of the gen.'

Cathie smiled from the carriage doorway.

'I'll do what I can. Goodbye, Alec, and thank you.'

Aunt Jean was bustling about the kitchen when Cathie arrived back at Barnside.

'There you are, dear. Keith telephoned and asked you to call him up when you got back. Have you had a nice day?' She didn't wait for an answer, but went pottering off into the scullery.

Cathie pulled off her hat, pushing back the unruly waves of dark hair.

'I went up to see Maggie. And I had lunch with Mrs. Chandler.'

'Very nice, dear,' a muffled voice said from the scullery. Aunt Jean came back carrying a large jug in a pan of hot water. 'Your uncle's got his cough again, so I'm making him some linseed tea. The man's a doctor, but he neglects his own ailments. "Physician, heal thyself",' Aunt Jean said tartly, spooning linseed and dried liquorice into the steaming water.

'Oh, dear, I am sorry. Poor Uncle Robert. Where is he?'

'He's sitting over the fire in his study like a bear with a sore head. And how I'll ever get this down him I don't know, but somehow I must.' She looked across to Cathie who had turned at the door. 'Don't bother him now, child. Go and call up your young man.'

'All right, Aunt Jean.'

Keith answered the telephone himself.

'Hello, sweetheart. I'm glad you're back at Barnside. What happened—did you go to a cinema?'

'I'm sorry you missed me before,' Cathie said. 'I went up to see Maggie. And then I missed my train.' She hesitated the fraction of a second. 'I met Alec Hamilton at the station and he insisted on giving me tea.'

'Good for him! He's the advertising bloke, isn't he? The one who's keen on your friend Sheila, or something? I've got some good news for you, Cath darling. I'll tell you about it properly to-morrow night, if you can meet me after the store closes. It's the chance to go into the office of Mr. Seymour, of Seymour &

Watkins. He's an old friend of Father's.'

'I know,' said Cathie slowly. 'It's wonderful news, Keith. I am glad. And you do deserve it. I met your mother in town, and she invited me to lunch and told me all about it. It was—it was very nice of her, wasn't it?'

Keith whistled.

'She never mentioned it. Expect she forgot. I'm awfully glad, Cathie. I mean, that Mother was so decent. I'm sure she'll come round. Especially when I join Mr. Seymour—we shall begin to see daylight then.'

'I'm glad, too,' Cathie said again. She wanted to ask about Melanie Seymour. She wanted Keith to mention her, to talk about her. She wanted to know if Keith still had any of that 'great interest' in her that Mrs. Chandler had spoken of. But she couldn't. I'm being awfully silly, she thought. She remembered Alec Hamilton's intent blue gaze across the station tea-room table. After all, people can be friends.

Evidently Alec Hamilton was of that firm belief. The next morning, at Stirling's, he appeared in the perfumery, and tracked Cathie down.

'Hi, there. Ready to give me a little assistance?'

'Of course,' said Cathie. 'What can I do?'

Alec waved to the hovering Miss Bentall, first

sales of the perfumery.

'That's all right, Miss Bentall, I won't take up your valuable time. Miss Munroe here can give me a price list and the few details I want.' He drew Cathie aside. 'We're going to do a Rose-leaf cosmetic column and a Fernley column, and one other, say Samarkand or Blue-mist. Will you give me some details of the various kinds of stuff they pack up? Skin food, cleansing cream, powder, and so on.' He smiled. 'How are you getting on here? Do you really like it? What I'm getting at is this—one of the girls in the Ad. department, a female called Margaret Green, is leaving unexpectedly. She does sketches and rough layouts. I was wondering if you'd like to come upstairs and join us? It's pleasanter than this racket. I can't guarantee anything, and I don't want to raise your hopes, but you mentioned something last night, when we were talking, about being keen on art?'

He paused inquiringly.

'But, Alec—in Advertising? I don't know the first thing about it.'

'Of course you do.' Alec laid a pad of paper on the counter in front of him. 'Look here! Here's half a column in a newspaper. Imagine we want to advertise Samarkand perfume, talcum, and say, bath salts. You rough out a flacon, a container or box for the powder, and a jar for the bath salts. Get it? Leave a space like this for the copy, that's the reading matter.' He made a few quick movements over the paper. 'Or here's a female going into the bathroom, one hand out to take down something from the shelf. A jar of bath salts, of course! And here's the talc.'

He pushed the pad across to Cathie.

'Will you rough out some ideas for me in your lunch hour? Or this evening? If you've any possibilities at all I think I can get you into our department. That is, if you want to come.'

Cathie flushed with pleasure.

'Of course I'd like to, Alec. It's something I've always been interested in.'

'That's the girl!' Alec said encouragingly. 'Do your best, Cathie, and I'll see what I can manage.' He turned away.

Cathie laid a hand on his arm.

'Alec, thank you. It's awfully good of you to take all this trouble.'

'We're friends, aren't we?' Alec said abruptly over his shoulder. He strode away.

Miss Bentall came fluttering forward.

'Now, Miss Munroe, I'm sure you can't make a price list for Mr. Hamilton on your own. Why, you don't even know the stock yet. What exactly does he want? He's always such an erratic young man, so unconventional.'

Cathie stared down the aisle after him.

'He's very kind.' She met Miss Bentall's blank stare. 'It's about the Samarkand line of cosmetics,' she said hastily. 'Also the Roseleaf and the Fernley.' She explained some of Alec's requirements to the anxious Miss Bentall.

She decided to say nothing to Sheila about the sudden opportunity Alec had given her, nor to Keith. It might all fall through. It would be better to raise no hopes until she had seen for herself what she could do.

She spent a happy evening with Keith, but left early to return to Barnside. Dr. Malcolm's cough was a little easier after a long-drawn-out argument with his wife, in which he had been defeated, and reduced to taking the linseed tea under her vigilant eye.

Late that night Cathie sat up, making sketches and drawings, and the next day she took them to Alec.

He looked at them but made very little comment.

'Thanks, Cathie. I'll show them to Mr. Wales, the Advertising Manager, and let you know what he says.'

CHAPTER 5

A FEW days later Cathie was surprised to receive a note in Mrs. Chandler's handwriting.

'Dear Catherine, If you are free on Saturday evening I should be very pleased if you would come up to dinner to meet our dear young friend, Melanie Seymour. Just a small, friendly party for seven-thirty p.m.——

Yours sincerely,
Gertrude Chandler.'

Cathie smiled wryly as she read it. 'Our dear young friend, Melanie Seymour.' Was it possible that Mrs. Chandler would refer to her, Cathie, in the same terms? 'Our dear young friend, Catherine Munroe.'

She shook her head slowly. No. Behind the politely formal phrases she sensed—what? A challenge of some kind?

Keith was delighted.

'You see, Cathie darling? Mother is coming round. And you'll like Melanie, she's a nice person.'

Cathie looked at him.

'She's—she's very beautiful, isn't she?'

Keith frowned.

'I suppose so. Divinely tall, divinely fair, that type.' He caught her wistful gaze, and pulled her up against him. 'Darling, I love you.'

'Oh, Keith, please don't stop. It all sounds so far away.'

He tilted her chin with one hand and smiled down into her eyes.

'What does?'

'The house in Henshawe Terrace.'

Keith laughed.

'Nonsense. It's much nearer, now that I'm lined up for Seymour and Watkins.'

Saturday evening was the worst possible time for a dinner party. Stirlings didn't close until six, and the whole of Saturday was one long rush of serving. There wasn't time to go out to Barnside to change, so Cathie had to pack a dinner dress in a suitcase and take it to the store, and manage somehow to change in the noisy, crowded cloakroom.

Sheila stayed behind with her. They could not linger too long at Stirlings, and when she was ready it was still too early, so they decided to go across to the Grand Central Hotel and have a coffee, and Cathie could add any finishing touches to herself there.

'What a lovely dress!' Sheila said admiringly.

It was a plain black nylon with lace insertion at the yoke. She cocked her head on one side. 'You look very sweet, Cathie, but a bit pale. What about some blusher?'

Cathie stared at herself in the mirror. She was well aware that after the long, rushed day in the busy shop she looked tired and drawn. There were smudged shadows under her deep blue eyes, and the black dress, although beautiful in itself, did nothing to add glow or life to her pale features.

She shook her head.

'I shall look like a Dutch doll, or someone with a fever. It makes me look artificial. I'll just have to be pale.' She smiled at Sheila. 'And interesting, I hope!'

At last it was time to go. She stepped into the taxi the doorman had whistled for, and said goodbye to Sheila.

'Thank you for waiting with me, Sheila. I'll see you on Monday.'

'Have a super evening!' Sheila called encouragingly from the pavement.

The daily help opened the door of Mrs. Chandler's house to Cathie and led her upstairs to leave her coat in her hostess's delicate rose furnished bedroom. As she opened the door of the drawing room for Cathie, Mrs. Chandler turned her head and saw her immediately.

'Catherine, my dear! How nice! I'm so glad you could come.' A smooth perfumed cheek brushed her own. 'Now, who do you know? Mrs. Cummings and Dr. Cummings—Miss Grainger. Now wait a moment, Keith, you shall speak to Cathie in a moment. Miss Munroe, Mr. Dale, Major Harmer. And this is Melanie. Catherine, my dear friend, Melanie Seymour.'

'Divinely tall, divinely fair,' Keith had said. 'Quite one of the most beautiful girls I have ever seen,' Mrs. Chandler had described her.

All the adjectives could be applied to Melanie Seymour. She was tall and statuesque; honey-gold hair woven in a coronet round a stately head; large, tranquil blue eyes, calm and remote upon Cathie; a complexion of roses and cream; perfect teeth showing in a small serene smile.

'How do you do?' A soothing phrase of sound in a low, sweet voice.

'How do you do?' Cathie echoed. She felt suddenly small and shrunken, a pale wisp of a creature in a black dress, standing before this glowing figure of cream and gold, whose white dinner-dress fell in folds of Grecian simplicity about her.

The daily help appeared in the doorway.

'Harold, please lead the way in to dinner with Mrs. Cummings,' Mrs. Chandler urged Mr. Seymour. 'Doctor, Miss Grainger. Mr. Dale,

Miss Munroe. Keith, you're to sit next to Melanie. Major Harmer, at this end, please.'

They were all settled, with Cathie between two strangers—Major Harmer, round and red-faced behind a bristling auburn moustache, and Mr. Dale, pale and scholarly with short-sighted green eyes.

She met Keith's look across the shining oval table. He smiled reassuringly, and her eyes warmed with affection.

Mr. Dale was a poor talker. After some heavy going she turned with relief to Major Harmer, who proved to be what he looked, a hearty sportsman.

'You play golf, Miss Munroe?'

'I used to play quite a good deal,' Cathie answered.

'Splendid. What club d'you belong to? I'm new around here, stationed temporarily, y'know. They tell me the Highfields is the place.'

'I used to belong to the Highfields,' Cathie said. 'It's very good.'

Mrs. Chandler leaned forward.

'Miss Munroe doesn't find as much time to play as she did, Major,' she explained carefully. 'She is one of our career girls. Aren't you, Catherine, my dear?'

Major Harmer chewed his duck industriously.

'Really? Working girl, eh? What d'you do?

Teach, nurse? I know—you're a secretary.'

Mrs. Chandler was being helpful again.

'Oh, no, Catherine is much more unconventional. She works in a shop. At Stirling's.' She smiled round at everybody in the sudden lull of conversation. 'In the perfumery department, my dear, isn't it?' She looked across the table, 'Melanie my dear, is it true you are going to assist Sir Spencer Brodie, the specialist, at St. Andrew's Hospital?'

'Yes, Mrs. Chandler. I'm to be his receptionist at his house and chauffeuse to and from the hospital.'

'Delightful! Such an interesting job.' Mrs. Chandler's glance slid over Cathie and dismissed her before returning to Melanie.

'I hear George Cross has opened his stables again, over at Longford. Keith, you will have to take up your riding again now Melanie is home to go with you. You were both so enthusiastic, and it did you both a great deal of good. After sitting at a desk all day it's just what you need.' Mrs. Chandler leaned towards Dr. Cummings. 'Doctor, is it true that riding puts ten years on to a man's life?'

Dr. Cummings laughed doubtfully.

'It may do, it may do. If he doesn't fall and break his neck and shorten it by ten years. Ha, ha, ha!'

The table joined in laughing agreement.

Cathie felt cut off from it all, from this smiling and assured group who were so familiar with each other. There was no one there she knew at all, only Keith and his mother. An odd situation. She knew so many people in Barrington she had quite expected to find some acquaintance at least here.

She watched Keith turn his head towards Melanie, saw him smile at her, and speak, and watched the slow, calm smile drift across Melanie Seymour's placid, beautiful face in return.

Then she became aware of Mrs. Chandler's watchful gaze upon herself. She met the impenetrable dark eyes for a second before Mrs. Chandler glanced away.

At last the seemingly endless meal was over. Mrs. Chandler rose and marshalled her guests back into the drawing-room.

Cathie found herself sitting on the sette beside Miss Grainger. She was a small trim woman with beautiful iron-grey hair and observant brown eyes. She began a discussion about plays, but as it was several months since Cathie had been to any shows, the conversation slowly petered out. Cathie felt flat and despondent. She could see her companion dismissing her as dull and somehow she no longer cared. She was tired, and something more than tired. She was—what?

Discouraged—defeated?

Someone came and stood beside the settee.

'Hello, Edith,' a slow voice said.

Miss Grainger swung her head round to smile with rekindled animation at Melanie Seymour.

'Melanie, my dear, how are you? I haven't had a chance to say a real hello. You're looking more glamorous than ever.'

'Thank you,' Melanie answered in her tranquil voice. She moved round and sat on the arm of the settee. Her serene smile included Cathie. 'You always say such flattering things, Edith.'

Miss Grainger nodded her head briskly.

'I mean them, too,' she said. 'Well, Melanie, how does it feel to be back in Barrington?'

'It feels good. All the nicest people I know live here, the ones I'm most fond of.'

'Thank you,' said Miss Grainger, 'though I doubt if you're alluding to me.' She turned her head obliquely. 'I scent romance. Isn't Keith Chandler one of your "nicest people"?'

'But of course,' said Melanie. 'Everyone is agreed upon that. That he's one of the nicest people.' Her blue eyes rested on Cathie. 'Don't you think so, Miss Munroe?'

Cathie felt herself colouring. She had not Melanie's calm composure. Cathie was usually vivid and alive, unless she was tired or unhappy. Emotion showed through her, chasing over her small expressive face as sunshine and shadow lighten and darken the heather-clad hills or sparkling streams.

She managed to say quietly: 'Yes, he is very nice.'

The drawing-room door opened and Dr. Cummings came in, followed by the rest of the party. Keith came straight over towards the settee.

He bent his head before them.

'I bow to the Three Graces.' His smile included them all, but it lingered on Cathie. His dark eyes sent a secret loving message. 'Darling,' they said.

The sense of tiredness lifted. Cathie smiled back, warmed and reassured.

'Were your ears burning?' Miss Grainger inquired. 'We were talking about you, Keith.'

'Nicely?'

'Oh, very nicely.' Miss Grainger smiled at her own joke. 'The nicest things.'

Major Harmer sauntered over, attracted by the laughter and not least by the glowing figure seated on the arm of the couch.

'So you're a horsewoman, Miss Seymour? Do a spot myself. Might fix something up between us some time. What do you say, Chandler?'

'I'm afraid I don't have very much time these days,' said Keith. 'Miss Munroe rides, too, don't you, Cathie?'

Cathie smiled agreement.

'I'm like you, Keith, I haven't very much time.'

'You're growing very stuffy,' Melanie protested. 'All work and no play, Keith. I'm going to alter some of that.'

Keith's eyes were on Cathie.

'Impossible. I've an object in view—something worth working for.'

'That sounds exciting. A secret,' said Miss Grainger smiling. 'What can it be, I wonder?'

The Major manoeuvred Melanie Seymour towards the further end of the room. Mr. Dale hovered towards them, a bewildered bird in search of a resting place. He perched himself happily upon the settee beside Miss Grainger and waited for her to encourage him with crumbs of conversation.

Keith squeezed Cathie's hand against the folds of her dress.

'What about tomorrow?' he asked. 'Can I come out to Barnside?'

'Oh, do,' Cathie urged in a low voice. 'Aunt Jean said you were to come any Sunday you wanted to.'

'That's every Sunday, then,' Keith answered.

Mrs. Chandler seeing the party break up into couples decided to rearrange matters and with skilful charm and diplomacy brought them all together again.

Cathie's train left at ten o'clock, so she was one of the first to leave. Keith wanted to walk down to the station with her, but Mrs. Chandler dismissed the suggestion by announcing that a taxi had already been ordered.

'To-morrow, then,' said Keith. 'After lunch?'

'I'll meet your train,' Cathie offered.

Mrs. Chandler had overheard. She came forward and put a thin white hand on Keith's arm.

'I'm afraid you will have to disappoint Catherine. Have you forgotten that we are going over to Mr. Seymour's for the day?'

Keith frowned.

'But I thought it was for supper—an evening arrangement?'

'Oh, no,' his mother returned lightly. 'Mr. Seymour is calling for us some time in the late afternoon.' She smiled sympathetically at Cathie. 'You must cancel your plans, I'm afraid, my dear. Keith will not have time to go out to Barnside.'

Cathie returned the smile politely.

'I quite understand, Mrs. Chandler. Keith can come over some other Sunday. Goodnight, and thank you so much for my pleasant evening.'

She turned with simple dignity towards the door.

Keith walked down the steps with her. He caught her arm against his side.

'It's a beastly nuisance. Sweetheart, I'm so sorry. It's nothing to do with me. What about Monday evening? No, that's hopeless, I've a lecture. Tuesday? Six-thirty at the Connaught?'

'That will be lovely, Keith. Goodbye, darling, and don't worry. I know—it's nothing to do with you,' Cathie answered wistfully.

He caught her up in a brief embrace, ignoring the taxi-driver's grin, then banged the door upon her.

'Nothing to do with you,' the throbbing engine seemed to say. 'Nothing to do with you.'

Only with Mrs. Chandler. Smooth smiling enemy; calculating foe.

They would have to have the most tremendous faith in one another, fight hard to disentangle themselves from the silken web of Mrs. Chandler's weaving. Against the moving screen of the night outside, Cathie seemed to see the figure of Melanie, seated on the settee like a queen on a throne, regal and beautiful. Sure of herself. She has everything, Cathie thought. All the weapons I once had. Money and background; the help and influence for Keith that his mother was so determined he should have.

The night sky was pricked with stars. Brightest and clearest shone Venus. As Cathie said goodnight to the driver and turned towards the station she looked up and saw it's glittering light. Her heart lifted and she thought, with some sense of comfort, Keith and I have our love.

CHAPTER 6

CATHIE was glad when it was Monday again. Sunday out at Barnside was happy enough with the kindly Nesbits, but there was too much time to think, to doubt in. Monday was the Store again—the bustle of people about one; a job to be done. What was it Carlyle once wrote? That 'work is the grand cure of all the maladies and miseries that ever beset mankind.' Cathie, stacking up neat pyramids of jars and bottles on the cosmetic counter, was inclined to agree with him.

Sheila came hurrying by, and managed to whisper to Cathie, 'Did you have a super time on Saturday?'

Cathie smiled round at her.

'Lovely, thank you.' Too involved to explain, to discuss with Sheila. But her heart warmed towards her, to the friendliness and comradeship she had found at Stirlings. This at least was real and worthwhile and to be cherished.

Halfway through the morning Alec appeared upon the scene.

'How's the Ad girl this mellow Monday?'

Cathie gave him a puzzled look.

'Didn't I tell you?' he said casually. 'You're lined up for the job.'

Cathie's eyes widened.

'Oh, no, Alec!'

'But yes. Mr. Wales wants to see you this morning. Will you go up about twelve—just before your lunch break? He'll have a chat with you, and arrange about your transfer.'

Cathie still couldn't believe it.

'You mean I'm really going to be in Advertising?'

Alec laughed.

'I feel just like Father Christmas, as if I'd given you the fairy from the top of the tree. You really think you'll like the change, then?'

'Oh, yes!' In Advertising! Drawing and sketching. Doing the sort of thing she had always had an intense love for. Something that wasn't work but was a part of herself. 'I'm going to love it.'

'So'm I,' Alec twinkled. 'It's going to be good to see more of you, Cathie.'

Cathie opened her mouth to speak, then paused abruptly.

'It's all right,' Alec went on. 'It's quite genuine. Old Wales thinks your sketches have what it takes.' He twirled imaginary moustachios. 'It wasn't just me powerful influences for me own fell purpose, m'gel.'

Cathie burst out laughing so that Miss Bentall, appearing unexpectedly from behind a tier of soap, frowned disapprovingly.

She had just time to whisper, 'You are silly, Alec. But I'll never know how to thank you.'

'Until the midnight hour,' Alec whispered, and loped off down the aisle.

Miss Bentall puckered thread-like brows suspiciously.

'What is it Mr. Hamilton wants this time?'

'It's about—about a transfer into the Advertising Department,' Cathie answered.

'Into Advertising?' Miss Bentall stared after Alec, then back to Cathie. 'How very extraordinary,' she remarked with powerful emphasis.

Mr. Wales, the Advertising Manager, was tall and thin with grizzled grey hair and the widest, thickest horn-rimmed glasses Cathie had ever seen.

He fingered the sketches she had done previously and gave her a friendly smile.

'You've quite a talent for sketching, Miss Munroe. Good balance and perspective. Do you think you can find a few ideas for us too?'

Cathie took a deep breath and said, as confidently as possible, 'I think so.'

'Good. There'll be plenty of openings for you here. I thought we'd start you on this side, general layout and ideas, and see how you go.

If you feel it's a bit beyond you you can be moved across to the studio, where it's drawing pure and simple. I'll have a word with Mr. Childers about it and see if we can't get you started up there tomorrow morning. How's that?'

'It sounds—ideal,' Cathie answered.

Hubert Wales grinned in friendly fashion.

'Can't offer you any substantial rise, I'm afraid. About the same as the perfumery at the moment. Say, a couple of pounds more as there's no commission.'

'Thank you,' said Cathie. 'Thank you very much.'

'OK, then. You'll be sharing an office with Miss Fanshawe and Terry Duncan.' He stood up and held out a long thin hand. 'Good morning, Miss Munroe.'

'Good morning, Mr. Wales.'

She walked jubilantly along the narrow passage where glass-paned doors led into the light square rooms of the Advertising offices. She caught glimpses of bent heads, drawing-boards, paint pots, sheaves of papers and sketches, galley proofs, typewriters. Everybody seemed busy and occupied.

Sheila was already in the canteen dining-room.

'Hello, what kept you?'

Cathie slid into the vacant chair beside her.

'Sheila, the most fantastic thing has happened. I hadn't time to tell you before, it all came up this morning.' She paused for breath. 'I'm moving up into the Advertising Department!'

Sheila halted with a fork in mid-air. She laid it down again on her plate.

'How on earth did that happen?'

'It was all through Alec,' Cathie explained. 'I mean—he suggested it. At the station when we met—' She broke off at the sight of Sheila's puzzled face. 'Oh, dear, I'm making a muddle of it. I'd been to see Maggie—'

She began at the beginning and told Sheila all about it.

Sheila's face was still puzzled.

'You—never told me,' she said slowly.

Cathie put a gentle hand on Sheila's arm.

'I didn't mean to hurt you, or be secretive. It seemed such a chance in a million that I waited for it to be more concrete before I said anything. Do you understand?'

'Yes, of course,' said Sheila. Her eyes were somehow questioning. 'Alec—he—he likes you a lot, doesn't he?'

'I think we're friends,' Cathie answered. She couldn't bear the bewildered look in Sheila's brown eyes. 'He—I've told him all about Keith, Sheila.'

Sheila brightened a little.

'Have you?' She began to eat her shepherd's pie again. 'You know, I'm awfully glad for you, Cathie. It's—it's terrific. And I'm sure you're clever at drawing. Mr. Wales wouldn't have given you the chance otherwise. I expect you're just what they want in Margaret Green's place.'

'Thank you, Sheila.'

Silence fell between the two friends. With all her heart Cathie wished Alec would fall in love with Sheila. If there's anything at all I can do to help, I'll do it, she thought. I like them both so much and Sheila deserves to be happy.

The next morning Cathie presented herself in the Advertising Department.

Once again there was that sensation of being a New Girl, like at school, Not knowing anyone or anything. A little lost, a little bewildered, standing around rather helplessly in the long narrow room which she was told Miss Fanshawe and someone called Terry Duncan occupied. Cathie had taken good care to arrive early and it seemed that she was too early.

A tall woman with a cloud of silver-grey hair around a startlingly young face came into the room, carrying a small attaché-case. She smiled at Cathie.

'Hello, you must be Miss Munroe. I'm Molly Fanshawe, woman's copy-writer.' She gestured towards a youth about nineteen with a snub nose and stiff upstanding brown hair who had come in behind her. 'This is Terry Duncan, he does some of the men's stuff. I think he's planning to do Alec Hamilton out of a job.' She smiled at him. 'Some day.'

She sat down at a desk at one end of the room. There was another desk at the other end and in between a rectangular table under the window. Molly Fanshawe waved a slender hand towards the table.

'Margaret sat there. Hope the light's all right. 'Fraid there's only one drawer to it, but you can stick anything you want in this cupboard here,' and she jerked her head backwards.

Cathie sat down at the table while Molly started to unpack the attaché-case and stow various things in the drawers of her desk. Then she stood up and took off her navy coat and ruffled up the silver-grey waves in a mirror on the wall behind the desk.

A head came round the door. It was Alec.

'Hi there!' His eyes warmed as he met Cathie's relieved gaze. 'Hail, Molly, and hail again, Terry. Molly, this is my favourite protégée, Cathie Munroe. I want you to take good care of her.'

'We'll do our best,' said Molly.

Alec came over and sat on the edge of Cathie's table.

'I must inform you that you work directly under me. Can you bear it?'

Cathie nodded happily.

'I think so.'

He pulled a sheaf of papers from his pocket.

'See what you can make of these. It's copy for the library. Molly here will explain anything you don't understand. We're getting out some bookmarkers, to be distributed inside the books. Try and think out some thumbnail sketches to go on them, humorous for preference.' He smiled down at her. 'Let me have something by to-morrow morning.'

At first it seemed as if her brain would never work. The longer she gazed at the copy the fewer ideas seemed to come. She stared out of the big window which was at roof-top level. The flags hung almost still from their posts in the quiet air. She turned and met Molly's look, smilingly sympathetic.

'Get something down,' Molly said, 'even if it's only a drawing of Mickey Mouse. You'll find it helps.'

She was quite right. The first few attempts were ruthlessly scrapped by lunchtime, but some ideas had come. The whole of the afternoon Cathie found herself working with absorbed interest and when she paused to breathe, it was six o'clock.

Never had a day gone so quickly. Cathie said good-night to Molly and Terry and hurried to the cloakroom to wash and tidy up before she met Keith at six-thirty. When she came out of the staff entrance she was surprised to find Alec waiting for her.

'Well?' he said. He shortened his long stride to hers. 'How did things go?'

Cathie gave an expressive sigh.

'I'll know tomorrow morning.'

Alec cocked a sandy eyebrow.

'Like that, eh? It won't seem so tough when you get into it. I've a feeling you're going to make good.'

Cathie smiled up at him.

'Thank you, Alec. You're always a most reassuring person to be with.'

'Am I?' He tucked a hand through her arm in friendly fashion 'Cathie, there's a staff dance at the beginning of December, on the eighth. Will you come to it with me?'

Through the foggy gloom she could see him staring down at her. She said slowly, 'Is it just for Stirlings' staff, or may people from outside come?'

Alec's voice sounded puzzled, as he answered.

'Oh, it's free-for-all. The staff can invite a friend to partner them. Is that what you mean?'

Cathie nodded.

'Yes, that's exactly what I mean.'

Alec stopped abruptly, his hold loosened on her arm.

'I see,' he said quietly. 'You want to ask Keith?'

'Yes.' She added quickly, 'Please don't be offended, and thank you for asking me. You've been awfully kind all along. But it wouldn't do, Alec.'

'Why not?' Alec demanded obstinately. 'I thought we were friends?'

'I'm engaged,' Cathie answered steadily. She went on hesitantly, 'Why—why don't you ask Sheila? We could make up a foursome?'

He laughed shortly.

'It's no use, Cathie. You can't matchmake me out of it. I like Sheila, she's a good sort. But it's you, you know.'

For a moment Cathie didn't answer. She looked up at him, caught the glint of his blue eyes under the street lamp, the burnished glow of his red head.

She said, 'Please don't, Alec. You said we'd be—friends. You're only making things difficult.'

'Sorry.' He reached for her hand. 'Look, if Keith can come I promise to invite Sheila. How's that? Am I forgiven?'

Cathie disentangled her fingers gently.

'Of course. Now I must hurry. I shall be late.'

'I'll walk along with you,' said Alec. 'Where are you heading for?'

'The Connaught Restaurant. I'm meeting Keith there. Please don't bother to come, Alec. It's out of your way.'

'No trouble at all,' he said gaily. 'I'll see you across the street anyway.'

The fog had thickened. They waited on the edge of the pavement until the blurred discs of a car's headlights had crawled past them. Another car hooted warningly. Alec took her arm again.

'Come on, over we go!'

They hastened across to the road island, then over on to the opposite pavement.

'Thanks awfully,' Cathie said breathlessly. She was about to say 'Good-night, Alec,' when a tall figure loomed out of the drifting vapour about them and said:

'Is that you, Cathie? I was beginning to worry about you.'

It was Keith. He came across to them, to stare down at her, and became aware at the same time of Alec, standing just behind Cathie.

'Keith, this is Alec Hamilton, from Stirling's. I've told you all about him. Alec, Keith Chandler.'

'How d'you do,' Keith said abruptly. He held out a stiff hand.

'How d'you do?' Alec replied. He added

casually, 'I was just seeing Cathie safely through the fog, but I must be on my way now.' He nodded to Keith, and gave Cathie a brief salute. 'Goodnight.'

They both called 'Goodnight' as the tall figure disappeared into the gloom.

'So that's Hamilton? You seem to be on very good terms.'

'We're friends,' Cathie said. 'Alec has been immensely kind to me.' She tucked her hand in Keith's. 'Come on, darling, let's go in and have something to eat. This damp fog makes me feel absolutely raw.'

The Connaught Restaurant was a bowl of warmth and light after the chill street. Cathie sat down at their usual table and took off her gloves. She smiled across at Keith.

'Hello.'

The frown on his handsome dark face lifted. He grinned suddenly at her.

'Hello.'

'That's better,' said Cathie. 'You looked quite ferocious.'

'I felt it,' Keith acknowledged. 'There was I waiting for my girl and getting all steamed up because you were late and along you came arm in arm with Hamilton. Lost in the fog.'

'On our way to you,' Cathie amended. She picked up the menu and studied it, then she asked, 'Did you have a nice time on Sunday?' There was a hint of laughter in her voice.

'Sunday? Oh, at the Seymours'? Yes, very nice, thanks. He came and fetched us in his car and took us for a run round first. Mother revelled in it. It was such a grand day.'

'Very nice,' Cathie observed. 'Your mother's awfully good-looking, isn't she?' she went on. 'Do you ever think she might marry again?'

'Quite often. In fact, she's had more than one chance, but she's turned them down. She once told me that her only interest in life was me.' He smiled ruefully. 'I wish she would pick on someone else. It's too much responsibility for one lone son.'

Cathie nodded.

'I know, darling. Perhaps she'll feel differently after you're married.'

'Perhaps,' Keith agreed. He leant back in his chair. 'Tell me all you've been doing, Cathie darling.'

Cathie hesitated.

'Well, I have some rather particular news. I've been moved up into Advertising.'

Keith lifted a surprised eyebrow.

'Advertising? That's rather sudden, isn't it? What happened?'

'Well, I—the chance of it was mentioned to me last week,' Cathie explained. 'But I didn't say anything to anyone in case nothing came of it. You know I've always been keen on sketching and drawing, Keith. I happened to mention it to Alec Hamilton, and he took some things I'd done to Mr. Wales, the Advertising Manager, and the next thing was they asked me to change over to that department.'

The frown was back on Keith's face.

'Hamilton? Of course, he's the advertising fellow. You really are getting awfully thick, aren't you?'

Despite herself the tell-tale colour flooded Cathie's cheeks. Remembering Alec's earlier invitation and the remarks he had made she couldn't keep the hint of self-consciousness out of her voice as she said, 'Don't be silly, Keith. It's all part of the job.'

'He seems to take an uncommon interest in you all of a sudden.' His eyes, black and angry, fastened on Cathie. 'I believe the fellow's in love with you.'

She coloured more furiously than ever.

'You're being ridiculous, Keith. We—we're just good friends.'

Keith was still smarting after seeing Cathie arm in arm with the perfect stranger who had turned out to be Alec Hamilton.

'Cathie, he's in love with you,' he repeated loudly.

Cathie glanced round, aware of interested ears and eyes.

'Please don't talk so loudly, Keith. You're making a mountain out of a molehill, and being very unreasonable.' Her own fears and doubts came flooding back to her. 'After all, if—if Alec is a friend of mine, it's no worse than the way your mother rams Melanie Seymour down my throat.'

'Melanie Seymour?' Keith echoed. 'What's she got to do with all this?'

'Only that I—only that you're such awfully good friends. You've always taken a great interest in her. Your mother told me so. She tries to make me jealous of her and I'm not. Only if you feel like that about Alec, whom I've only met at work, how do you suppose I feel about you and Melanie?'

She broke off and they stared at one another in silence across the square of tablecloth.

'But we're quarrelling,' Cathie said wonderingly.

They had never quarrelled. Always between them had flowed love and trust and harmony. Always each had known that the other put him or her first in their heart.

Keith reached abruptly for her hand.

'I'm sorry, darling. I've acted rather stupidly. Of course, you're bound to make all kinds of friends I can't know, or share with you. It's only that I love you, Cathie. I want to be first—always.'

'You are first,' Cathie said gently. 'I know I'm silly, too, about Melanie. Only she's so gorgeous, like a goddess.'

Keith smiled.

'And who wants to love or marry a goddess?' He gave a shiver. 'Too cold!'

She said, suddenly reassured, 'Oh, Keith, I've just remembered. Stirling's are having a staff dance in December and outside people are allowed to be invited. Will you take me to it?'

'Of course I will. It'll be great! When is it?'

'I think it's the eighth of December,' Cathie said. She waited expectantly.

'The eighth?' Keith repeated. He frowned. 'Are you sure? Oh, gosh, I don't think I can manage it. I'm—I'm tied up that night, Cathie. I was going to tell you.'

'Is it your work? Will you be away?'

'No. It's something I can't get out of,' Keith said. 'Mother accepted for both of us. We're invited in a party. It's the St. Andrew's Hospital Ball and I've promised to take Mother and go with her and Melanie and her father in a party.'

CHAPTER 7

For a moment Cathie could not speak.

One half of her wanted to shout out at Keith —'You can't go. You mustn't! Can't you see what's happening? Can't you see what your mother is trying to do? She wants to part us. And she will do unless we're careful. Unless we're as clever as she is.'

But the other half of her said, 'Be calm. Be reasonable. Keith's going to a dance. What of it? Supposing you go to the dance at Stirling's with Alec? Does that alter your love for Keith— or his for you?'

Keith's dark eyes were worried and unhappy.

'Cathie, you do understand, don't you?'

Cathie reached out her hand to touch the lean brown fingers on the tablecloth. She nodded.

'I—want to, Keith. Only——' She looked away in despair. How could she say, 'Only you'll fall in love with Melanie—as your mother wants you to.'

She did trust Keith, with all her heart. Only forces, deep and dangerous and beyond their control, were working against them.

'I shall hate it, Cathie, without you. But it's a charity affair. Mr. Seymour has taken tickets for a big party and Mother accepted for us both before I'd even heard a word about it. It's difficult to get out of.' He frowned. 'I mean, he's been so decent—offering to take me into his firm. It's my big chance, Cathie darling. It's our big chance. My final is in March—that means if I get through and join Seymour & Watkins there's every hope of us getting married before the end of next year.' He smiled across at her. 'D'you see, sweetheart?'

Cathie managed to smile back.

'Yes, of course I see. I suppose I'm being silly feeling—I don't know—sort of frightened.'

Keith looked puzzled.

'Frightened? Of what?'

'I don't know. Just—oh, I wish it was March and your examination was over!' She wanted to add, 'I wish you hadn't accepted Mr. Seymour's offer. I wish we could be independent.' But she didn't.

Keith was trying to reassure her.

'Honestly, Cathie, it won't be so long now. I've four more months to slog away in. If I pass, we're in the clear.'

'And if you—fail?' Cathie said slowly.

If you fail, months more of it, she thought. Of Mrs. Chandler's scheming. Melanie and her father—smiling and smooth. Uncaring.

'I shan't fail,' Keith answered steadily. His fingers closed tightly over her own.

What's the matter with me? Cathie thought. She took a grip on herself.

'Of course you won't fail. Forgive me, Keith darling.'

But some brightness had gone out of the evening. A shadow, slight, almost imperceptible, fell between them like a sword.

They went to the cinema for an hour or so, then down to the station for Cathie's train.

'I'm going to be pretty tied up in the weeks ahead,' Keith said. 'March is the deadline. I've just got to be on top of it all by then. You'll understand, darling, if we can't meet quite so often.'

His eyes were fast on Cathie's. 'Have faith,' they pleaded. 'Help me. Believe in to-morrow.'

Cathie reached her arms up about his neck, oblivious of the other passengers standing about the damp, ill-lit platform. Where, for that matter, did she and Keith ever meet, except in cafés and cinemas and shops and stations, with an occasional visit at week-ends to Barnside?

'Darling, I do understand,' she said softly. 'If we never meet at all I shall go on loving you— and believing in you.'

Keith held her close for a brief moment, his

cheek pressed close against her own. The whistle piped; the train gave an abrupt shudder. Cathie stepped back into the darkly chill compartment, waving from the window until Keith's tall figure was engulfed in the foggy gloom.

At Barnside a letter was waiting for her from Tom. He sounded immensely busy and engrossed in his new life, but happy and full of spirits.

'Thought you'd be married by this time [he wrote], but it's good to hear you're well and happy with Uncle Robert and at the new job. Sounds terrific. Wouldn't old Grandpa Munroe turn in his grave to think of you at the rival store!'

Perhaps Tom had read between the lines of her last letter and sensed something of the doubts and uncertainties of Cathie's future. He went on more seriously,

'You know, Cath, if things don't quite work out as you'd hoped I can raise the fare for you to join me here. I think you'd like it. Hills purple with manuka, and a tang in the air. Steve and I aren't lined up to be millionaires yet, but we're keeping our heads well above water.'

Cathie laid down the letter wistfully. Darling Tom! She missed him very much. They were

separated by so many miles. But her life lay here
with Keith now.

Next morning the fog had lifted. Cold bright
sunlight filled the streets, there was a nip in the
air. The winter trees in the park were black
etchings against a blue sky—white frost bordered
the grass. Above the cream stone of Stirling's
front yesterday's limp flags fluttered bravely in
the breeze.

Cathie's spirits seemed to soar as the lift
ascended. By the time she had reached the
Advertising Department and had been greeted
with Molly Fanshawe's friendly smile and Terry
Duncan's lopsided grin, she felt much better.

She finished the first rough sketches for the
bookmarks by the middle of the morning. Molly,
after a brief glance through them, told her to
take them to Alec in his office.

Alec turned round from the desk he was
standing against at her tap on the door.

'We-ll, look who's here!' His eyes, vivid and
intense, probed her own as he took the sketches
from her hand. 'No, don't go. I'd like to discuss
them when I've had a look-see.' He turned back
to the untidy spread of papers before him.

The sloping desk went the length of one wall.
Cathie stood uncertainly at his shoulder. Through
the wide windows she could see the jumble of
shops and roofs and houses broken by church

spires and clock towers that was Barrington. Somewhere below the river glinted.

'Umm!' Alec swung round. His broad shoulder brushed her arm. 'Not bad, Cathie. Not bad at all. You can go right ahead with these first two—draw them out properly and accurately, ready for photographing. The third one is a bit corny—nursery rhyme characters have been overdone. What about something on the grotesque? Quaint—fantastic. You want a good caption—maybe I'll think of one.' He smiled suddenly. 'But don't worry. You can't be perfect first time out, but you're doing all right.'

'Thank you,' Cathie said. She moved away.

Alec blocked the way.

'Don't go,' he said again, then—'Have a good evening?' he added casually.

'Very nice, thank you,' Cathie answered calmly. 'We went to see *The Lion in Winter*. It was very good.'

'I thought so, too,' said Alec. He looked down at her. 'Your young man seems very nice. Almost good enough for you.'

'Thank you.'

'Did you mention the dance?'

Despite herself Cathie's face clouded.

'Yes. I'm afraid Keith can't come. He—he has another arrangement that particular evening.'

'Splendid!' Alec cried. 'I hope that means you'll come with me.'

Cathie shook her head.

'No, Alec. Thank you very much, but—no, all the same.' She glanced up at him. 'Take Sheila,' she urged.

Alec shook his head too.

'Uh-uh. That wasn't the arrangement. You said if you didn't go with Keith you'd come with me.'

Cathie smiled.

'You said that, Alec. I honestly mean "No." If you really want to please me you'll invite Sheila.'

'For heaven's sake, why?' Alec burst out. 'I do want to please you, Cathie, but I'm not going to be pushed off on to Sheila. If you won't come with me I shan't go. So you needn't think that by refusing you're doing your friend Sheila any good. What about it? Say yes, please,'

Cathie moved round the desk towards the door.

'No, Alec. I—' She met his stare. 'I'm only encouraging you,' she protested.

'Fine. That's just what I need—a little encouragment.' He saw her begin to frown, and said quickly, 'Look, Cathie, don't make it a final "No" yet. You might change your mind. Let me ask you again later.' He patted her arm.

'And now, don't let me keep you, Miss Munroe. Thanks for the drawings.'

Cathie smiled ruefully to herself as she walked back to her own office. Alec was very difficult to argue with. You couldn't be cross with him, but she was determined not to accept his invitation. Keith wouldn't like it. His arrangements had been made by his mother. Cathie's would be made by herself. It wasn't on.

She really enjoyed working in Advertising. It was not nearly as tiring as her previous work down on the busy, teeming ground floor, with its constant flow of customers.

That evening Sheila walked part of the way with her to the station.

'Are you coming to the Staff Dance?' she asked Cathie.

Cathie shook her head.

'I don't think so, Sheila. I asked Keith to take me, but he's tied up that night.'

She saw Sheila's quick, sideways glance.

'I expect you could find another partner.'

Cathie knew she meant Alec. She was so fond of Sheila, she wouldn't do anything that hurt her. Remembering Alec's persistence all she could say was:

'I'll come another time with Keith.'

The bright day had darkened into a clear frosty night. It seemed as if every star was out, twinkling in the deep velvet blue of the sky. Barnside lay still and silvered with frost as Cathie walked up the flinty hill from the station to the main street. Lights shone out from the houses on to the pavement—a small boy went whistling by. From somewhere a radio was playing pop music.

Outside Dr. Nesbit's house an unknown car was standing. Visitors! Cathie opened the front door and went in. As she closed it behind her someone came quickly down the staircase. She glanced up but instead of Uncle Robert or Aunt Jean she saw a perfect stranger. He placed a black case on one of the hall chairs and lifted the telephone receiver.

'Barrington 8175,' he said authoritatively. He gave Cathie a preoccupied glance. 'Hello, St. Andrew's Hospital? This is Dr. Glover. Put me through to the house surgeon.'

Cathie stared. A sudden chill of foreboding swept her. She ran up the stairs to be met by Mrs. Nesbit on the landing. Aunt Jean put her finger to her lips.

'Ssh, dear. Your uncle, I'm afraid—' Her mouth puckered. She seemed to make a great effort. 'I'm afraid he's very ill, Cathie.'

Cathie's arm slid round the suddenly bowed figure. She helped her into the nearby bedroom and closed the door.

'What is it, Aunt Jean, darling? What can I

do to help you? What is it? Tell me—'

Mrs. Nesbit turned bewildered eyes upon her.

'The—he collapsed. On the way home from Matthews' farm. He'd been up to see Mrs. Matthews and the new baby. He said he didn't feel so well at dinner-time, but I didn't take any more notice than usual. I know he's felt queer this long time since, but I thought it was over-work—that he's been overdoing things. They found him at the car wheel, blowing the horn to attract attention. Dr. Glover came over from Fernham. He says—he thinks—there's got to be an immediate operation.'

Cathie knelt beside her, rubbing the chilled hands between her own.

'That must have been Dr. Glover telephoning the hospital just now. Try not to worry, Aunt Jean. He'll be all right, I'm sure he will.'

Aunt Jean glanced helplessly about her.

'They're sending for the ambulance. I'm going with him, Cathie. I must. I must be there —when——' She broke off, but no tears came.

'Of course,' Cathie said. 'Come along, dear. I'll get your things. I'll pack a suitcase for us both.' She helped her aunt to her feet and opened the door.

Doctor Glover came up the stairs. He gave Cathie a quiet smile.

'Good evening. The ambulance will be here in about twenty minutes or so. Will you be ready to leave, Mrs. Nesbit?'

Aunt Jean nodded.

The district nurse came out of Dr. Nesbit's bedroom and made a gesture towards Dr. Glover. With a brief 'Excuse me' he followed her into the room, with Mrs. Nesbit hovering at his heels.

Cathie began hurriedly to put some things into a suitcase. She went downstairs and saw Mrs. Nesbit's daily help. She gave her some instructions and promised to telephone any further news. Then she returned upstairs in time to see Dr. Nesbit lifted on to a stretcher by the two ambulance men. He was unconscious, his usually florid face drained of colour.

Mrs. Nesbit clutched at Cathie's arm on the way into the street.

'It's his heart, Cathie, I'm worrying about. I'm so afraid—under an anaesthetic——'

Cathie helped her up into the ambulance.

'Uncle Robert's got a wonderful constitution. He'll be all right, I'm sure he will, darling. Try not to worry—you'll have so much to do later.'

It seemed an endless journey. At last they were standing outside the massive bulk of St. Andrew's Hospital, its windows forming rows of yellow light against the darkness.

Dr. Nesbit was placed on another stretcher and wheeled away into a lift and up to the operating theatre.

A kindly Sister led them both to a waiting-room. She smiled gently at them from the door-way.

'Don't worry,' she said reassuringly. 'There may not be any news for some little time, but I'll come and tell you just as soon as it's over.'

Minutes seemed like hours. Time ticked by in a small isolated world of waiting. Beyond the door footsteps hurried past; a tinkling trolley rolled up the corridor. There was a low murmur of voices as some unknown engaged another in conversation.

Aunt Jean seemed to have shrunk. Her plump prettiness, her happy bloom had vanished. She sat on the striped rust and blue of the armchair staring down at her folded hands, speaking in a vague manner to Cathie, who did her utmost to distract her troubled thoughts.

A young nurse came in carrying a tray of tea. With her entered anew the sounds and smells of the hospital.

The door closed after her.

Aunt Jean stirred her tea slowly.

'I should be used to all this. It's been part of my life for forty years. Hospitals and operations —doctors and nurses.' Her pinched mouth trem-

,bled. 'But when it's your own—lassie——'

Cathie reached a hand out.

'I know, Aunt Jean.'

Aunt Jean stared up at the ceiling as if trying to see through it.

'They've been so long. It's past nine o'clock.' She turned to Cathie. 'What a good girl you are. Where'd I have been without you today? You're like a daughter to me.'

The door opened and Dr. Glover stood there. He came straight over to Mrs. Nesbit and laid his hand on her shoulder.

'It's over,' he said. 'Dr. Nesbit stood up magnificently. It's been a big job, but his pulse is steady as a rock—there's every chance he'll be out of the wood in a few days' time.'

Aunt Jean was crying quietly into her handkerchief. With one free hand she caught Dr. Glover's and clasped it for a second, then let it go.

Dr. Glover turned to Cathie.

'Were you intending to return to Barnside?'

Aunt Jean answered for her.

'I'd prefer to be within call. I want to be with him just as soon as he can see me.'

Dr. Glover nodded.

'I understand. A room in a hotel is the best thing. The Crescent, a road or two away from here, is extremely good about keeping an odd

room for us for these emergencies. I'll get someone to ring through for you.'

'Oh, thank you.'

'Thank you very much, doctor,' said Cathie.

Accommodation was found for them—a small
room which they must share. Neither of them
felt in the least like eating, but a light supper of
cold meat and potatoes, salad and apple pie was
served to them in the deserted dining-room. They
then went slowly upstairs to bed.

When Cathie was undressed and Aunt Jean in
bed, she went over to the window and opened it,
drawing back the curtains a little. The lights of
Barrington twinkled around them, the blue-
white glow from the main street stretching
threadlike into the distance. A clock chimed
somewhere nearby. Half-past ten. A few hours
ago she had been working at Stirling's. She and
Aunt Jean had lived a lifetime in half a day.

To-morrow she would telephone Keith. Perhaps he would have time to call at the hotel
while they were there.

She crossed over to the bed and laid a kiss on
Aunt Jean's cheek.

'Goodnight. Try to sleep. The worst is over
and to-morrow you'll be able to sit with him for
a little while, perhaps.'

'Goodnight, my dear. God bless you,' Aunt
Jean said.

CHAPTER 8

FIRST thing in the morning Cathie put a phone call through to the hospital and received the usual assurance that Dr. Nesbit was going on as well as could be expected.

It was arranged that Mrs. Nesbit would be able to see him for a little while around eleven o'clock. Cathie promised to return to the Crescent for her lunch break and would then hear any further news from Mrs. Nesbit herself.

Alec met Cathie in the corridor of the Advertising Department.

'Just the person I was looking for,' he said heartily. 'I've got an idea for that third bookmark—the time factor. People always say they have no time to read. What about all those odd minutes wasted in buses and trains, or waiting in queues?' He broke off, suddenly aware of Cathie's pale face and shadowed eyes. 'Cathie, you look awfully under the weather. Is anything wrong?'

'No—yes—I mean, not with me,' Cathie told him. 'But with my uncle, Dr. Nesbit, whom I'm staying with. He was taken seriously ill yesterday evening. He was rushed off for an operation. He's safely through it, but it's a very anxious time for us, for a day or so.'

'I'm sorry,' said Alec. His voice was deep and warm and sympathetic. He put a hand under her elbow. 'Come in here and tell me all about it.'

Cathie walked through into his office where she told him some of the happenings of the evening before.

'I do hope your uncle will be all right,' Alec said earnestly. 'Look, would you like the day off? I think I can wangle it for you.'

'No, thank you, Alec. There's nothing I can do. Aunt Jean will be at the hospital on and off all day, but they won't let me sit with Uncle Robert as well. I think I'd rather keep on working.' She looked up at him. 'It's very sweet of you. You're being very kind.'

'Nonsense.' His fingers touched her own for a brief second. 'It's just that, if there's anything I can do, you will remember—friends?'

'I'll remember,' Cathie promised. Alec's immense vitality, his obvious admiration, flowed over her in a soothing current. Difficult to resist Alec, if you'd been in love with him. Only she wasn't. She said, with an attempt at briskness, 'What about those sketches? You mentioned the time aspect. I think it's a good idea.'

Alec took his cue, moved over to the desk

against the wall.

'Something on these lines,' he suggested, holding out a square of paper.

It was lunch-time before she realised. The Crescent Hotel was a bus-ride away, but Alec had assured her that she was not to feel tied for time or worry about being late.

Aunt Jean was waiting for her in the dining room. Her bright blue eyes filled with tears as she said, 'You'll never guess what his first words were. I'd been sitting there, still as a mouse, just watching and waiting. Suddenly, he was looking at me, his eyes as wide and sensible as your own. He said, "Don't fret yourself, Jean. We'll be having that holiday away, down in London, we always promised ourselves."'

She dabbed quickly at her eyes, then blew her nose. 'He fell asleep again quite soon. Oh, but he looks poorly, Cathie.'

'I'm sure he does,' Cathie said consolingly. 'But he'll pull through now, Aunt Jean. He'll be all right, and won't you have a lovely holiday?'

'He's fretting. He said have they got me a locum, Jean. I'll have to speak to Dr. Glover. Your uncle will never make progress if he's worrying about the practice. Now, dear, eat your dinner. Don't sit there staring at me. I'll be all right. I just can't help going on about poor Robbie.'

'I was offered the day off. Would you like me to ask for this afternoon?' Cathie asked. 'I could stay with you.'

'No, my dear. I'll be at the hospital. I'll have a word with Dr. Glover and set your uncle's mind at rest if he happens to come to and ask me again while I'm there.'

'I'd like to telephone Keith and tell him what's happened. He'll be so sorry. Perhaps he'll come down to the hotel tonight.'

'Hurry away, dear. Do just that,' urged Aunt Jean. 'He's bound to want to be here with you at such a time.'

The number was engaged. Somebody came and stared impatiently at Cathie in the telephone booth. She quitted it, only to find her successor was bent on making a lengthy trunk call.

It was no use. She must wait until later in the day. Cathie returned to Mrs. Nesbit and said goodbye, then hurried away to the nearest bus stop.

When she got back to the hotel at night, Aunt Jean was sitting in the small lounge, talking to a tall, thin young man.

He stood up as Cathie came over to them.

'Cathie dear, this is Dr. Peter Lang. He's taking over for your uncle. He's been a doctor in the army and has been out in Vietnam, but he's been invalided home for a while. Now your uncle won't worry a minute longer and it's a great load off my mind.' She finished with such a deep sigh of relief that both Cathie and Dr. Lang smiled and met each other's glance in mingled amusement.

Cathie put out her hand and received a firm handshake.

Dr. Lang's eyes were grey in a thin, pale face. He could have been any age between twenty-eight and forty-five. It was difficult to say. He had deep lines about the eyes and mouth, and an air of controlled tension. He looked as if he had suffered a great deal of pain. When he smiled he gave the impression of being younger and very sweet-natured.

'They're very pleased with your uncle,' Aunt Jean said, when Cathie asked after him. 'He's making good progress. Dr. Glover says he'll be round the corner by Sunday and then it's just a question of nursing and the long convalescence.' She smiled across at Dr. Lang in a motherly fashion. 'So our worries will be over, if you're able to stay on.'

'I'm a free agent,' Dr. Lang answered. 'I'm only too happy to take over for as long as Dr. Nesbit wishes.' His deep-set eyes twinkled. 'Unless he wants to get rid of me in a hurry!'

'You're not in practice on your own, then?'

Cathie inquired.

'No. As a matter of fact, I've had a long bout in hospital myself. The effects of dysentery and fever. It was suggested I had better confine myself to locum work and so on for at least six months before tackling a job abroad again.'

'I see.'

Aunt Jean struggled up out of the armchair.

'Come along, Cathie. We were waiting for you. Dr. Lang is having dinner with us so I can explain one or two matters to him before he goes out to Barnside. Mrs. Crackan will look after him until we get back there.'

There was no help for it. She would have to phone Keith after dinner now.

At last the meal was over. While Aunt Jean ordered coffee, Cathie hurried to the phone booth at the back of the hotel.

Mrs. Chandler herself answered the call.

'Catherine, how very nice! How are you, my dear?'

Cathie masked her impatience as she made a few polite remarks.

'Keith—I'm so sorry, Catherine, I'm afraid he is out. Perhaps I can take a message for him.'

Cathie hesitated. She said slowly, 'I'm telephoning from the Crescent Hotel. My—Dr. Nesbit, whom I've been staying with, is in St. Andrew's Hospital after a serious operation.

Mrs. Nesbit and I are staying here until Sunday. I wonder if you would tell Keith.'

Mrs. Chandler's voice flowed smooth sympathy over the wires.

'My dear, how dreadful! I am sorry. It must be most worrying for you and for Mrs. Nesbit. I do trust Dr. Nesbit will make good progress.'

'Thank you, Mrs. Chandler.'

'Most certainly I will give Keith your message. What a pity he is out for the evening. As a matter of fact, he has gone to some little party somewhere with Melanie Seymour. I think you have met her. Of course, here at my house.' Mrs. Chandler's light laugh echoed across the distance. 'Goodbye, Catherine. I do hope all will go well with Dr. Nesbit. Be sure to let us know.'

'Thank you,' Cathie said again. She stood staring down at the smooth black shape of the telephone receiver in her hand. She replaced it gently on the holder.

First the hospital, now this. It was just an unhappy coincidence. It didn't mean anything. It couldn't. Keith had been trapped once more into some invitation against his own wishes. Mrs. Chandler's softly malicious voice—'Some little party somewhere.'

The remembrance of Keith at the railway station only a night or two ago.

'I'm going to be pretty tied up, Cathie, for

the next few weeks.'

Not sufficiently to exclude Melanie Seymour.

Cathie clenched her hands despairingly. 'This is when I wanted Keith so much—when I needed him. What am I to think? What am I to do?'

When Cathie returned to the lounge, Aunt Jean was pouring out the coffee. 'Well, dear, is Keith coming down to join us?'

Cathie took her cup in one hand. She shook her head. 'He's out, Aunt Jean. I spoke to Mrs. Chandler. She said she would give him my message.'

Her voice sounded flat and empty. She seemed drained of feeling and effort, as if she had surmounted a series of rising slopes only to find the hill ahead rising as steep and menacing as ever.

She saw Aunt Jean glance anxiously across at her and was annoyed with herself. This is no time to worry about my own affairs, Cathie told herself. When Uncle Robert is so ill and Aunt Jean so troubled. She managed to smile reassuringly. 'Keith will be here tomorrow I know.' She turned to Dr. Lang. 'Is your home in Barrington, Doctor?'

'My parents live some way outside, nearer Corston to be exact, but I know Barrington fairly well. I trained at St. Andrew's Hospital.' His smile included Mrs. Nesbit. 'It's a fine place, one of the best equipped hospitals we have. Dr.

Nesbit wouldn't get better attention anywhere.'

'I'm sure of that,' Cathie agreed.

'As a matter of fact, I'd intended to come back there and specialise—in glandular diseases. It's one of the big things of the future. The medical profession is still only on the fringes of it.' The grey eyes lit up into gentle laughter. 'That's the particular bee in my bonnet, Miss Munroe. We all have one, you know. Mine's glands.'

Cathie's first instinctive liking for Dr. Lang deepened. She smiled back.

'I wonder what mine is, or Aunt Jean's?'

'I know what your Uncle Robert's is,' Aunt Jean said tartly. 'It's the practice. The practice and the patients morning, noon and night. His wife and his home come a poor second and it's no wonder he's so neglected himself that he's lying, half dead, across the way there.' Aunt Jean's voice faltered at the end and betrayed the emotion masked by her sharp-sounding words. 'Be thankful you are marrying a lawyer, Cathie, and not a doctor.'

Dr. Lang raised one eyebrow. 'You're engaged to be married, Miss Munroe?'

Cathie felt herself colour. 'We—we have no actual plans yet. It's just—just a sort of understanding.'

'Away with you,' Aunt Jean cut in. 'You and Keith are like two plants without water when you're out of one another's sight!' Her blue eyes twinkled towards Dr. Lang. 'I know a love match when I see one. What of yourself, Doctor? Are you heartwhole and fancy-free, or are you hoping to find yourself a nice wife when you set up on your own again?'

Cathie scarcely heard the doctor's reply. She was thinking of Mrs. Nesbit's remark. 'Plants without water when you're out of one another's sight.' Perhaps that had been true of them once, but was it now? Time and circumstances, the influence of outside people, seemed to be conspiring to sever those first close links—the intertwining of their two lives. Against her every effort of trust and belief, clamouring fears and doubts, like invaders, battered at the door of her heart.

Dr. Lang was standing up.

'I think I should be getting along, Mrs. Nesbit. Now please don't worry yourself in any way about the practice. I'll telephone you every day to set your mind at ease, until you're able to return to Barnside.' He bent his lean height over her outstretched hand. 'Goodnight, Mrs. Nesbit. Goodnight, Miss Munroe.'

'Goodnight,' Cathie echoed. They watched him stride away across the room.

Aunt Jean settled herself down again with her knitting. She sighed, pursing her lips over a dropped stitch. 'Poor lad, he's been through a lot—it's there in his eyes. But I'm glad he's come to us at this time. Your uncle is going to take to him, I know that.'

'I like him too,' Cathie agreed.

Keith telephoned in the middle of breakfast next morning.

'I'm awfully sorry about Dr. Nesbit,' he said. 'How is he now? I do hope he's going on all right.' He sounded ill at ease and awkward. 'Cathie, I would have rung you last night, but it was—rather late when I got back. I hope you understood. It was something I couldn't get out of.'

Cathie tried to make her voice warm and easy, but the sentences emerged stiff, somehow disapproving.

'I understand, Keith. Don't worry about it.'

'I'll be down this evening, Cathie.'

'I may not be here. I may have to go to Barnside. Aunt Jean's got a locum in and some query has arisen out there.'

He didn't believe her. He thought she was making an excuse. But it was true. Aunt Jean had started worrying in the night about some papers of Dr. Nesbit's—about a list to be given to Dr. Lang. To set her mind at ease and enable her to go off to sleep again, Cathie had suggested that she herself should go over on the train, after she left Stirling's that evening, and settle any outstanding problems.

The telephone was like a barrier between them, hiding the real Cathie and Keith from each other, making them two embarrassed strangers.

'Well, I'll try and manage lunch-time,' Keith said.

It's all terribly difficult, Cathie thought, as she hurried back to her meal. Something is happening to us, and we can't seem to stop it. Keith is going one way with his mother and the Seymours, and I'm going another.

She thought that afresh as she entered the store and felt herself caught up in its immense machinery, once inside you were part of something so much bigger than yourself. Personal worries seemed dwarfed. She had felt it once before and she felt it again now, that there was relief and comfort in the interests of a job.

This is beginning to be my life now, Cathie thought as she watched the floors disappearing below through the iron gates of the staff lift. This is what matters. Everything else seems unsatisfactory except this.

As she stepped out of the lift, Alec came round the final bend of the stairs.

'Phew!' he puffed. He paused to get his breath. 'What news—how is your uncle? Is he better?' He tucked his arm in hers in such a consoling way Cathie could not find it in her to protest.

'I telephoned before breakfast and the Sister said he'd passed a satisfactory night—whatever that means. Anyway, if he has no relapse, every day after the operation counts for him. My aunt has gone over to sit with him again this morning.'

'Good,' said Alec. He scrutinised her face. 'You look a little better too—not quite so peaky. I can see you possess a nose and mouth this morning. Yesterday I could only see two enormous eyes!'

Cathie laughed and pulled her arm free at the door of her office. She didn't meet his look.

'We've got a locum for my uncle,' she said irrelevently. 'A Dr. Peter Lang. He's very nice.'

'Good,' Alec said again. 'What about lunch? Are you going back to the hotel?'

'I hope to,' Cathie answered. 'If—if I could have a little extra time.'

'Of course,' Alec assured her. 'Take what you want.'

'Thank you, Alec.'

Molly Fanshawe was already in. She gave Cathie a warmly, sympathetic smile. 'How's the patient today? I do hope it's good news.'

'My uncle is making good progress. We hope he'll be round the corner by Sunday.'

'I'm so pleased. I understand just how you feel, because I remember what a dreadful cloud I seemed to live under a year ago when Trudy was ill in hospital.'

'Trudy?' Cathie echoed questioningly.

'My little girl.' Molly laughed at Cathie's expression. 'You look so surprised. Didn't I tell you?' She sat down at her desk and rummaged in her handbag. 'Here she is.' She held out a snapshot. 'It was taken six months ago. She's fine now.'

Cathie stared down at the thin, elfin face before her. She looked very like Molly. Her hair was an aureole about her head—only it appeared to be blonde, where Molly's had turned to premature grey.

'She's sweet,' Cathie said warmly. 'And so like you. But I'd no idea—that you were married, I mean.'

'I'm a widow.' Molly slid the photograph back into her bag. 'Jack was an airline pilot. His plane crashed about two years ago.'

Cathie hardly knew what to say. 'I'm so very sorry——' she began.

Molly reached forward and patted her hand.

'Don't grieve for me,' she said. 'I'm over it now, Cathie. It was one of those unbearable bits of life that no matter what, you have to live through. But I'm adjusted now. I have Trudy and I have wonderful memories of my life with Jack. We had the most tremendous fun and happiness together in the few short years we were married. Now I've my job. I still think I'm luckier than most people.'

'You're awfully brave,' Cathie said.

Molly smiled. 'It's not brave to accept the inevitable. That's just common sense.'

CHAPTER 9

When Cathie returned to the Crescent Hotel at lunch-time, Mrs. Nesbit met her excitedly in the hall.

'Come along, Cathie,' she urged. 'If you hurry, we'll have time to slip over to the hospital. Dr. Glover says you can just peep in at your uncle if he's awake. Two minutes, he says, just to say hallo.' She sat down at their usual table in the dining-room. 'He looks better this morning. I think he has a better colour. Of course, he's terribly weak. He can't talk or anything, but he lies there and watches me in between a little doze or two.' She sighed. 'He seems more like my Robbie.'

'That's wonderful,' smiled Cathie. 'And of course I'd love to see him for just a minute.' She thought about Keith. He might be here at any moment, but he would understand. Perhaps he could walk over to the hospital with them.

Mrs. Nesbit and Cathie hurried through their meal. Every time the dining-room door opened, Cathie glanced up expectantly, hoping to see Keith. They finished eating and were ready to leave and still he had not come.

Depression was a damp cloud settling about her. It's no use, Cathie told herself. I don't want to be unreasonable, but it's so awful to keep counting on someone and to keep being let down.

The hospital had a different kind of atmosphere in the daytime. Bright sunlight filtered through the long corridor windows, dispersing the shadows of fear and anxiety that crowded upon one in the long night hours of waiting.

Dr. Nesbit was in a small private ward at the bend of a long corridor. He was propped up against high pillows, his eyes closed. Cathie looked down at his crossed hands on the coverlet and felt love and pity flood her heart at their unaccustomed helplessness and thinness.

Aunt Jean sat down on the edge of the chair by the bedside and at the same moment Dr. Nesbit opened his eyes. Without moving his head, his eyes turned to smile at her. He said, 'Jean.'

Aunt Jean laid her hand over his. 'How are you, Robbie? Here's Cathie come to say hallo to you.'

His gaze travelled round to Cathie as she bent towards the bed.

She put one finger to her lips. 'Don't tire yourself talking, darling. I'm so glad you're better. Don't worry about Aunt Jean—I'm taking care of her. Just get well.'

He smiled. 'Good girl!'

Cathie laid a kiss on the top of his head. 'Darling Uncle Robbie!'

He touched her terribly—suddenly so much an old man and yet, strangely, so much a sick small boy lying there—striped flannel pyjama jacket and untidy, damp grey hair, framed by the pillows. He had closed his eyes again in weakness. Cathie tiptoed away, signalling to Aunt Jean not to move.

Outside in the corridor she stood blinking her eyes a minute beside the half-open window.

A car swung through the iron gates into the courtyard below. A little group of people got out —a short man in a black felt hat, a big well-built man with white hair, two women, one slim and grey-haired in grey tweeds, the other tall and statuesque with plaited coils of blonde hair.

Cathie stood, transfixed, by the window, staring down at them as they moved towards the doorway.

Because there was one more person in the group, and he was Keith. Mr. Seymour and Melanie, Mrs. Chandler and a stranger, and Keith. They were coming here into the hospital.

Her only desire was to escape them, not to be confronted by that assured, compact little group, not to face Keith as he apologised or made excuses under his mother's softly mocking eyes.

Cathie turned to hurry away down the corridor. The hospital was a vast building and they
might not be coming in this direction, but she
was taking no chances.

As she reached the top of the stairs, someone
called, 'Miss Munroe!' and Dr. Peter Lang
came over to her.

'Good afternoon. I expect you're surprised to
see me here, but as it happens, I've been in to
see one of Dr. Nesbit's patients. How is your uncle
today? I was hoping to have a word with Mrs.
Nesbit.'

He stood staring down at her. Cathie thought
how grave and serious he looked without his rare
smile.

'She's sitting with the doctor at the moment,'
she answered. 'I think he's making good progress,
but he does seem awfully weak. I'm sure Aunt
Jean will be pleased to see you. She's been
worrying about one or two little matters,' she
added. 'In fact, I'd intended coming out to
Barnside tonight on account of them.'

'I'll have a word with her,' Dr. Lang promised.

The gate of the automatic lift rattled open.
Several people came out. Without turning her
head, Cathie was suddenly aware of who they
were. She moved a little and there was Keith,
waiting to catch her eye. He stepped forward,

but his mother was before him.

'Catherine, my dear! How fortunate to have met you like this. Before I say a word, how is Dr. Nesbit? I do hope you have a good report of him.'

Cathie shook the outstretched hand. 'He's going on fairly well,' she said in a low voice.

Mrs. Chandler gestured about her with grey suede-gloved hands.

'You remember Melanie and her father.' She turned her head. 'Oh, Sir Spencer has gone on. I would have introduced you. Melanie works for him, you know. Such an interesting man—quite brilliant. He has kindly offered to show Mr. Seymour and myself over the new wing that has just been completed. He insisted on Melanie driving us all over in his car.' Her gaze rested questioningly on Dr. Lang.

'Mrs. Chandler, this is Dr. Peter Lang, who has come to take over my uncle's practice for the time being.'

Mrs. Chandler's deep, dark eyes swept over the spare, unsmiling figure before her

'How do you do. How very nice of you. What a pity Barnside is such a dull little place to do locum work in. Miss Seymour, Dr. Lang—Mr. Seymour, my son Keith.'

In the general conversation that followed, Keith moved round to Cathie's side. 'Hallo,

Cathie.' It was odd how his eyes—so dark, so unhappy—could be like his mother's—and yet very unlike.

'Hallo,' Cathie said.

'I'm sorry I missed you at the Crescent.'

'It doesn't matter.'

'They told me you'd left. I came straight over. Melanie passed me on the way and gave me a lift.'

'It doesn't matter, Keith,' Cathie repeated silently. 'It just doesn't matter any more—nothing matters. You're always coming or going with them. It's always your mother, or Melanie, or her father.'

She turned her face away from Keith's pleading gaze and made as if to speak to Dr. Lang.

Dr. Lang was talking to Melanie. He was smiling, and the years and the sadness had slipped away from him again. He was gazing at Melanie.

'You, too,' Cathie thought sadly. 'Yes, she is very beautiful.'

There could be no greater contrast than between these two. Dr. Lang with his thinness, his greyness, his nervously taut air, his look of a man who after long confinement is let out into the bright light of day, and Melanie, golden and glowing, placidly serene, calmly content, entirely sure of herself.

'Melanie dear, Harold—Sir Spencer will wonder what has become of us. We mustn't keep him waiting. Goodbye, Catherine. It's so heartening to hear Dr. Nesbit is making a good recovery. Good afternoon, Dr. Lang. Keith, are you coming with us?'

'No, Mother, I haven't time. I have to get back to the office, after I've had a word with Cathie.'

'As you wish.' Mrs. Chandler led her little retinue away.

Dr. Lang gave Cathie a brief smile, nodded to Keith and disappeared along the corridor, towards Dr. Nesbit's room.

Cathie and Keith were left to themselves. 'About last night——' Keith began.

'Please,' Cathie said, 'I don't want to hear. I'm sure you couldn't help it, but I haven't time to discuss it. I have to get back to Stirling's.'

Keith caught her arm. 'You're annoyed about it. I suppose you're annoyed about lunch-time, but honestly, Cathie, I was held up at the office. It was nothing to do with my mother and—and Melanie and everybody. Please try and understand.'

'I do understand,' Catherine said in a low voice. 'I'm beginning to understand much more. For instance, just how hopeless it all is.'

Keith stared at her. 'Hopeless?'

Cathie gestured despairingly. 'I think I'm beginning to lose faith, Keith. We've so much against us. I don't think I can go on fighting your mother.'

Keith's eyes widened 'Mother? What's Mother got to do with it?'

Cathie turned away with a shrug.

'You can't see, Keith. You can't see the wedge she's driving between us. I've tried to withstand her, but it's no use. She's putting me in an awkward position—as a sort of hanger-on. I'm allowed a little of your time when she and Mr. Seymour have finished with you.'

'That's not true, I've been working,' Keith burst out. 'I have my exam.'

Cathie shook her head sadly. 'No, Keith, not always. And when you're through your examination, what lies ahead? The partnership with Mr. Seymour and his firm. Can't you see where that will lead? The drift away and the excuses.'

'You're imagining things. You're being unreasonable. Mother isn't like that.'

Cathie bit her lip. 'Of course I'm being unreasonable. That's just what your mother wants you to think.' Her breath caught on what might have been a sob. 'It breaks my heart to say it, Keith, but it's no use. I can't go on. I see too clearly the way it's all going to end, and there's one thing your mother can't take away from me

—and that's my pride. I'm giving you up.'

Keith's dark gaze held her own. 'Cathie!'

Cathie couldn't bear it. She nearly flung herself into his arms crying, 'I love you, Keith—I love you so much.' Then the accumulation of the past weeks, of the past months, seemed to swamp her like a wave. The memory of that evening with Mrs. Chandler, with the first threat behind her smooth, smiling words, when she learnt of the Munroe bankruptcy, returned. The smiling dinner party when Cathie had met Melanie.

She managed to say, 'I've got to go, Keith. It's late.'

'You can't go like this. I won't let you go. Cathie, listen to me!'

She flung away from him. A white-capped Sister came down the corridor towards them. At the same time, the lift door ahead opened to let someone out. Cathie ran forward to the lift. She pulled the gate to and, through a haze of tears, fumbled for the button marked 'Ground Floor'. Keith's voice echoed down the shaft after her. 'Cathie, Cathie, wait!'

She was crying as she hurried out of the hospital gates, along the road to the bus stop. She blinked back the tears with an iron effort.

'I just can't go on,' she told herself over and over again. 'I can't, it's no use. Mrs. Chandler has won.'

She was calm again by the time she reached Stirling's.

Molly Fanshaw and Terry were both busily working in the office. Molly gave her an absent-minded smile and went on typing.

Cathie sat down at her own desk and pulled forward the rough sketches she had been busy on. Her brain felt stupid. She was unable to concentrate. She found herself doodling vaguely and shading in bits here and there.

It couldn't really be over between herself and Keith. Did she really mean it to be? And yet was there any other solution? The end would be the same, whatever she did. Mrs Chandler would distort and poison Keith's mind so that he would see Cathie as his mother wanted him to see her—as someone jealous and possessive and unreasonable. He would seek an escape from her in the end.

What was it that Molly had said earlier that day? One of those unbearable bits of life that no matter what you have to live through. Molly's had been a tragic sorrow, but it seemed as if these heartaches, greater or less, came to everyone.

'It isn't brave to accept the inevitable,' she had said. 'It's just common sense.'

The door opened and Alec came in. He crossed over to Cathie.

'How's the bookmark coming? Finished yet?'

Cathie shook her head. 'Not quite—I'm—I shan't be long.'

Alec picked up the top piece of paper. He stared down at the scribbles, the rough outlines and vague spheres. He whistled.

Cathie tried to look away. She pulled the paper from Alec's hand. 'That isn't the one.'

'Bring your stuff along to my office. I think I can help you out with it,' Alec said quietly.

Cathie picked up the sheaf of papers and followed him out of the room along the passage. He pulled open his door for her and she went in and stood by the long desk rather uncertainly. Alec came and stood at her elbow. 'What's wrong?' he asked gently. 'Is it your uncle?'

Cathie shook her head. The kindliness and concern in his voice made her unable to speak for a moment.

'Look,' Alec went on, 'I thought we were friends. Can't you tell me?'

Cathie swung round.

'I've broken my engagement,' she said.

CHAPTER 10

THERE was a short silence. Neither of them moved.

'Why?' Alec asked gently.

A gull wheeled away in the distance—blown paper against the winter sky.

Cathie raised her hands in a gesture of helplessness. 'I—can't explain, Alec. It's so terribly involved. Perhaps—some time.'

Alec came to her side. 'I don't want to pry, Cathie. Only to know if you mean it.'

Cathie did not meet his look. 'I mean it, Alec. I—If you still want me to come to the Staff Dance with you, I will.'

'It's a week today,' Alec said matter-of-factly. 'I've got a car and I could come out and collect you from Barnside.'

'Oh, you needn't bother,' Cathie said. 'I can come in on the train.'

'Rubbish,' said Alec. He smiled. 'It's a special occasion—the first of many, I hope. We can fix times later. It's enough to know you're coming with me, Cathie.' He picked up the papers she had brought in. 'Like me to finish this for you?'

Cathie shook her head. 'No, Alec, that's my job. I—just wasn't able to concentrate. I'll have another go at it.'

'Good girl! Look, take a walk round the store. Get a fresh angle on things. It'll help. And I'll hang on to these for a quarter of an hour or so and rough out a couple of ideas.' He added hastily, 'I'm not going to do it for you.'

Cathie smiled gently. 'Thanks, Alec. You're—you're very kind.'

She walked slowly along the corridor and down the stairs. Household Furniture was a desert of tables and chairs and bedroom suites with a few shoppers scattered along its aisles. A fair, bespectacled youth and a little dark-haired girl were pricing hearthrugs. You could almost read their thoughts as they glanced at one another above its rolled-out length. Two armchairs on either side of a glowing fire, the hearthrug between them, the television set switched on; home—their home.

Cathie hurried on. Wherever you went, people were planning, hoping and dreaming.

Downstairs to the fourth floor, the third, the second. On the first floor, Sheila was waiting for the lift to come up. She smiled at Cathie in surprise.

'Hallo, stranger. What are you doing here? I missed you at lunch. How is Dr. Nesbit,

Cathie?'

'He's heaps better. I saw him today for a few minutes.'

'Oh, I am glad!'

'I'm looking for inspiration,' Cathie went on. 'I was stuck and Alec suggested a walk round.'

'Good idea,' Sheila agreed. Her observant brown eyes saw Cathie's face cloud again after the effort of animation. 'How's Keith?' she added.

Cathie met her look with steady eyes. 'I— we've quarrelled, Sheila—for good. It's all over between us.'

'Why, Cathie——' Sheila began. She broke off. 'I'm sorry.'

'Thank you.' Cathie went on staring at her. 'Sheila, Alec has asked me to go to the Staff Dance with him and I've accepted. I—hope you don't mind.'

Sheila's smile remained as friendly as ever. 'Why should I mind? Alec and I are only good friends.' Her chin tilted a little. 'I've known he liked you, Cathie, right from the start.'

Wherever you went, Cathie thought again, people were planning, hoping and dreaming and wherever you went, somebody's dream was being shattered. I'm shattering Sheila's, yet what can I do? If I don't go with Alec, he still won't fall in love with her.

'Here's the lift,' Sheila said abruptly. 'Going up?'

'No, down,' Cathie said in sudden relief.

Life was a muddle. Sheila liking Alec and Alec liking herself. Keith, Melanie and the endless conflict with Mrs. Chandler.

Only it's finished now, Cathie thought, making her way along the ground floor, unaware of the throng of busy shoppers around her. She squared her shoulders unconsciously. I'm putting it behind me.

Easy to say. Heartbreakingly difficult to do, when there was a letter from Keith waiting for her at the hotel later in the day. Weakness flooded her when she saw the dearly familiar writing.

'Cathie my darling, I know you were upset today at the hospital, but I know, too, you couldn't really mean all you said. I love you, Cathie, with all my heart. Please believe me and please let's forget all about this afternoon. I've got to be out of town until tomorrow evening, but I'll come down to the hotel just as soon as I get back. If you've returned to Barnside, I'll be out on Sunday. All my love, sweetheart, always,

Keith.'

She stood staring down at the letter in her

hand. If Keith had walked in there and then and taken her in his arms, there would be nothing more to say because love was a flooding heart-ache inside her. 'Oh, Keith,' whispered Cathie. A tear fell with a large plop on to the paper, smudging the firm writing, which seemed to be Keith's voice speaking to her.

She read the letter through again. 'Out of town till tomorrow night.' Business reasons, of course. Something to do with Keith's firm. But there had been too many excuses lately.

What would be the use of giving way to Keith's pleading and to the foolish prompting of her own heart, only to find later on that things were no better, that his mother's schemes still held him back!

The hotel bedroom was empty. Aunt Jean must still be at the hospital. Without daring to hesitate, Cathie sat down at the small table in the window and opened her leather writing-case.

It seemed queer to be calling him, 'Dear Keith,' as if he were little more than a stranger.

'Dear Keith, [Cathie wrote quickly]
    'I meant every word I said to you this after-noon. Please don't try to see me, or come out to Barnside. This is really goodbye between us. You'll realise I'm serious when I tell you I've accepted Alec Hamilton's invitation to

Stirling's Dance, and shall now feel quite free to accept all future ones. Please believe me when I say I wish you every good fortune.' She signed it formally, 'Catherine Munroe.'

It was done. She had burned her boats behind her. There was no going back. Alec was thrust between them—an unsurmountable barrier.

Cathie sealed down the envelope and hurried down to the hall where a postman was emptying the last collection from the posting box into his sack. The letter was tipped into it, lost in a tilting cascade of other letters. The postman tipped his cap to Cathie and to the girl in the office and disappeared through the door as Mrs. Nesbit entered it.

'Cathie, my dear! Were you wondering where I'd got to? I stayed late with your uncle because it's all arranged—we're going back to Barnside tomorrow night.' Mrs. Nesbit tucked a plump hand through Cathie's arm and added rather breathlessly, 'So you must come straight home from the shop.' She glanced sideways at Cathie's still face and added, 'Your uncle's making fine progress.'

Cathie forgot her troubles in Aunt Jean's delight. 'I'm so glad! Isn't it marvellous he's got on so well? I told you he would, Aunt Jean.'

'So you did. So you did.' Aunt Jean swept a brief glance round their shared bedroom. 'I'm not saying we haven't been comfortable here, but I'll not be sorry to be back in my own home. Dr. Glover says another week at this rate and your uncle will be able to come home himself to us. He'll be under Dr. Lang, so we'll have no need to worry.'

'That's splendid,' Cathie said. She added, 'I've accepted an invitation to go to Stirling's Staff Dance next Friday. That's a week tonight. I thought you'd be able to spare me by then.'

'You could go this very night,' Aunt Jean said warmly. 'You're not to stop all your pleasures for us, especially now your uncle's going on so well. But I thought Keith wasn't able to take you.'

'I'm not going with Keith,' Cathie said slowly. She hesitated. She wanted to explain how things were, but the words wouldn't come.

Mrs. Nesbit looked at her with sharp, shrewd blue eyes. 'You know best, my dear.'

'Thank you.' Cathie turned to the dressing table and made as if to brush out her curly dark hair.

It seemed strange the next evening to return to Barnside and find Dr. Lang sitting across the tea-table opposite her, while Auntie Jean was in her usual place. But he was so simple and friendly. He had such a quiet sincerity of manner that in no time at all it seemed as if he was one of the family.

'This is a fine old house,' he said to Mrs. Nesbit. 'Very real and solid and—what's the word—at peace. As if it had seen a great many comings and goings. Is it very old?'

'Around two hundred years,' Aunt Jean answered. 'It belonged to the Nesbit family quite half of that time. There's been three generations of doctors in this house. My husband and his father and his grandfather.' She glanced about her. 'I'm afraid it's not very up to date, but I'm most attached to it.'

Dr. Lang nodded.

'I might have guessed. It has an air of continuity.' He pulled out his pipe and looked across at Mrs. Nesbit. 'May I?' and at her nod, proceeded to light it. 'That's what life lacks today,' he went on thoughtfully. 'Continuity. A sense of things being tomorrow what they are today and what they were yesterday.'

He met Cathie's serious, absorbed gaze and smiled his sudden, transfiguring smile. 'What I'm trying to say is how very much I like it here —how very much I'd like to be able to stay on.'

'I thought you were going to specialise,' Cathie said.

He shrugged.

'Yes, later on. But I'd like to find somewhere where I could settle. Maybe for a time, or maybe for always—where I could still study.'

Mrs. Nesbit was watching him carefully.

'Dr Nesbit will be looking for a partner, I imagine,' she said slowly. 'He'll never go back to do the work on his own.' She became aware of the implication of her words and added quickly, 'But it's not for me to settle the doctor's business.' She picked up the silver tea-pot and hot-water jug and hurried out of the room.

Cathie and Peter Lang met each other's eyes across the shining table. Cathie thought with surprise that already he looked better—more rested. The deep lines about his mouth seemed softened in the lamplight's glow.

Three generations of Nesbits in this house. It was sad to think Uncle Robert had no son. Who would be here when he had gone? This quiet old stone house wanted someone like Peter Lang. Someone who would appreciate its slow stability, who would be patient and kind with the country people around him, who would appreciate their regard for the old doctor and their distrust of brisker, more progressive ways.

Sunday morning broke bright and clear as a spring day. Only the sharp frost was December's. The sun shone down on the whitened fields. The tufted grass on the roadside stood stiffly upright against a rigid patterning of fern and bracken.

Mrs. Nesbit and Cathie walked down the street and across the narrow, stone bridge towards the church. The river flowed smooth and dark between its banks. Birds, cattle and trees were black silhouettes against a silver background.

Mrs. Nesbit was full of plans to make a temporary bedroom of Dr. Nesbit's study.

'We can see that he is kept quiet and yet he'll be in touch with us all. He'd like that, Cathie. You know what he is. Every time the doorbell goes or the telephone rings, he'll be calling down to know who it is. Now, if we bring the oak bedstead down from the side bedroom, he'll be able to lie quietly there and hear for himself without fussing and fretting about what's going on. Maybe after dinner you'll give me a hand, and perhaps Dr. Lang would help us with the bed.'

'Of course,' Cathie agreed, as they went into the church.

Cathie knelt down in the cold little church and thought about Keith. Sometimes it was difficult to know how to pray—whether to pray for a miracle that everything would turn out right somehow in the end—that Mrs. Chandler would relent or Keith inherit a legacy to make him independent, or something equally wonderful and impossible—or one could pray for courage, for trust and faith, for a belief that in the end things worked out for the best.

'Help me do the right thing,' Cathie prayed. 'Help me to have patience, not to be bitter or to hate Keith's mother. She thinks she's doing the right thing too. She thinks she's helping Keith.'

It seemed muddled and unsatisfactory, but somehow she felt more at peace as she and Mrs. Nesbit walked slowly home, held and buttonholed many times on the short journey by enquiries after Dr. Nesbit.

Dr. Lang came in from his rounds just as Mrs. Crackan carried in the Sunday joint. His pale face had a little colour in it this morning, due to the cold and zestful air outside.

After a short rest, they all set to to rearrange the study as a bedroom.

'Once I get the bed up in here, it'll be easy to fix the rest,' Mrs Nesbit said breathlessly. She seemed to have forgotten that the doctor wouldn't be there for another week. 'Mrs. Crackan will give it a good clean round tomorrow, or maybe Tuesday. Tomorrow is wash day. Oh, thank you, Dr. Lang. Put it here, will you.'

'I wish you'd call me Peter,' said Dr. Lang, struggling with the long iron bars. 'I feel really one of the family now.'

'I'd be glad to,' Mrs. Nesbit said. She pushed a small table into the window recess. 'Now we've more room. I'm sorry to have troubled you on such a day, Dr.—Peter, I mean,' she amended quickly. 'But I couldn't have rested until I'd seen how it was going to be.'

'I'm glad I was here to help,' Peter Lang said. He glanced at his wrist watch. 'We've timed it nicely, because I'm due out now.'

'It's never a call on Sunday afternoon,' Mrs. Nesbit cried. 'You'll have to plan your days better than that, I'm thinking.'

Peter Lang smiled, but his eyes were grave.

'It's pretty important. Farmer Moore's little boy, over at Starlings Wood—he's had some ear trouble and I'm frightened of mastoid complications. I want to check up on him again or else get another opinion. It may mean hospital for him.'

'I know the Moores,' said Mrs. Nesbit. 'Robin's the idol of their lives. Hurry away with you, Peter. We'll have some hot tea and a good fire waiting for you when you get back.'

Peter smiled at them both and went quickly away. A minute later they heard the engine of the car spluttering and choking into motion.

It was five o'clock before they heard the crunching of the car wheels over the hard, frosty ground in the yard at the side of the house. The car door banged and Mrs. Nesbit looked up at Cathie in surprise as they heard voices on the step outside. Mrs. Nesbit stood uncertainly up and crossed to the drawing-room door. A gust of cold air swept through the hallway as the heavy front door closed behind Peter Lang.

'Hallo, Mrs. Nesbit. I hope you won't mind, I've brought you a visitor.' He turned to the tall, fur-clad figure at his side. 'I wonder if you've met before. This is Melanie Seymour.'

Cathie stood in the doorway, a little behind Mrs. Nesbit. Over her aunt's plump shoulder she stared in surprise at Melanie Seymour's beautiful face.

Melanie stepped forward. The shining pelts of her fur coat framed the coils of gleaming gold hair and a complexion brilliant from the frosty air outside.

She said, 'Please forgive me, Mrs. Nesbit, my car has broke down just near the bridge and I was struggling with it when Dr. Lang came along. I wonder if I might telephone for a taxi or something. I'm on my way to fetch Sir Spencer Brody from his country house and he'll wonder what has happened if I'm late.'

Mrs. Nesbit gestured towards the telephone in the hall.

'Certainly. Use it for whatever you want. I don't know quite where you'll get a taxi at this time of day, though.'

Melanie Seymour smiled. 'I think Turner's in Barrington will find someone. They know Sir Spencer very well.' She met Cathie's gaze. 'Why, Catherine, how very nice! I do hope you remember me.'

Cathie nodded. 'Yes, of course I do.'

Peter Lang was searching through the directory.

'Here we are, Melanie. Barrington 84211. Shall I try and get them for you?'

Melanie Seymour's eyes of tranquil blue stars bent upon him. 'Please do.'

Mrs. Nesbit and Cathie turned back to the drawing-room and waited by the fire until the murmur of voices outside had ceased. Then as Peter ushered Melanie into the room, Mrs Nesbit rose and said, 'Will you have some tea while you're waiting? It won't be a second, the kettle is on for Dr. Lang.'

Melanie sat down in the proffered chair and unfastened the rich brown coat.

'Thank you so much—if you're sure it's no trouble.' She shook her head at Peter Lang's cigarette case. 'No, thank you. I seldom smoke.'

Cathie went quietly out of the room and helped to make fresh tea. She thought how strange it was that Melanie was here. She was beautiful. It was obvious already that Peter Lang was attracted to her.

Tea was over and a rattle at the front door announced a hire-car driver from Turner's garage. Melanie turned and thanked Mrs. Nesbit most graciously for her help and hospitality. Then she smiled at Cathie and at Peter Lang with equal friendliness. She said, 'I'm so glad to see you again, because I was wondering about something. There's a big dance at St. Andrew's Hospital next Friday and if you aren't already engaged, my father and I would be very pleased if you would join our party and come along with us.'

She waited expectantly.

For one wild moment, Cathie thought, Keith has asked her to do this. It's his way of making amends because of my letter. Then she thought, No. Keith would ask me himself. Melanie had some other motive.

Melanie was smiling at her.

'I'm very sorry,' Cathie said slowly. 'I already have an engagement for that evening.'

'What a shame!' She turned to Peter Lang. 'And you, Doctor?'

Peter Lang's thin face was alight. He looked young and alive again.

'Well, I'm free,' he said diffidently. 'If you want a spare man.'

'But of course,' said Melanie. 'That's super.

Will you come to the house first for sherry?
Eight o'clock—we're all meeting there. Goodbye, Mrs. Nesbit—Catherine. I hope we'll meet
again. It's too bad you can't join us on Friday.'

CHAPTER 11

MELANIE turned serenely away towards the steps and Peter Lang followed after her to the car door. Arrangements had been made to tow Melanie's car into Barrington in the morning.

'There's a good-looking girl,' Mrs. Nesbit observed as she and Cathie started to clear away the tea things. 'Like a—like a film star.'

'Yes,' Cathie said. She was thinking that she could have gone to the hospital dance after all and Keith would have been there. Perhaps it was just a large, informal party. Perhaps he was just one of many. She gave herself a little shake. It's over and done with. No use starting all over again. I'm going to the dance—to Stirling's dance, with Alec.

Alec was quite firm about coming out to Barnside in the car on Friday to take Cathie to Stirling's.

He arrived about seven-thirty, looking taller than ever and immaculately well-groomed and clean-cut in his dinner jacket.

Aunt Jean fell for him at once. She bloomed under the spell of Alec's charm like a young girl.

Her look said to Cathie, 'Well! No wonder you're not going with young Keith.'

Cathie was determined to enjoy the evening. She was determined not to think about that other dance being held just across the town. She was wearing a new dress she had bought specially—a deep midnight blue chiffon, which darkened her own blue eyes to an almost violet colour.

Alec was extravagant with compliments.

'You're perfect, Cathie,' he said. 'A beautiful little pocket Venus. I adore you!'

He sighed so exaggeratedly that Cathie wasn't in the least bit embarrassed and was able to laugh at him as easily and delightedly as Alec always made her do. It was wonderful too to be admired—to be made to feel that Alec's evening was crowned because of her.

The dance was being held in Stirling's chief restaurant, known as the Tudor Hall. The room had been strikingly decorated with massed chrysanthemums and a specially augmented dance band was playing from a gallery at one end of the hall.

Sheila was there, shiny brown hair and bright brown eyes above a scarlet dress. She said, 'Hallo, Cathie. Hallo, Alec. Isn't it terrific here tonight?'

Alec beamed down upon her. 'Don't forget to

save me a dance.'

'I won't.'

Cathie wanted to put her hand out to Sheila, wanted to say, 'Sheila, it isn't my fault, honestly.'

Molly Fanshawe came up to them, her silvery hair swept up above a turquoise blue dress. She looked thin and fragile and yet oddly attractive. She was dancing with Hubert Wales. They all stopped to chat for a few moments.

'May I have a dance, please, Miss Munroe?'

It was Terry Duncan, brown hair slicked damply across his broad forehead, round eyes gazing admiringly at Cathie.

'Of course, I'd love to, Terry.'

At supper, they shared a table with Molly and Mr. Wales and Sheila and her partner—a man from Window Dressing.

The evening seemed to be flying by. Everything was a whirling kaleidoscope of music and sound and light and laughter. Cathie was saying, for the hundredth time, 'Yes, I'm having a super evening.'

Of course she was having a wonderful time. No time to think—to regret it. No time for doubts or fears.

'Look,' Alec said plaintively, 'I'm the one who brought you here—your partner, remember? Here you are turning out to be the belle of the ball and I can't get a look in!' He pulled her hand through his arm and held it firmly. 'Come along.'

'Where are we going?' Cathie protested.

'Ah,' Alec breathed, 'now I have you in my clutches!'

Cathie giggled. 'Alec, you're so silly!'

Alec pushed open a door. 'Here we are. Perfect peace and quiet.' He released her arm and Cathie found herself in a small room that had a vague air of familiarity to it. She looked round.

'Staff Manager's,' Alec said briefly. 'Just the place for a private interview.'

Cathie stood quite still. The Staff Manager's office. What years ago it seemed since that day of her first interview—the day she had found her job at Stirling's. She had been so proud and pleased and full of hope.

Alec came and stood opposite to her.

'This really is a private interview, Cathie,' he said. His voice was suddenly very quiet and serious. He took her hand in his and stared down at the curling fingers in his own. 'Cathie— darling, darling Cathie. You know how I feel about you—how I felt since the day I saw you at the station. I told you I didn't want to pry, but I want you to tell me one thing. Is it really finished between you and Chandler?'

Cathie held her breath a moment. Alec's long

fingers tightened on her own.

She said, 'I—we've broken it off. It's over, Alec.'

'That's all I want to know,' Alec answered. 'Just to know if you're free, Cathie, because I'm asking you to marry me. Next week, next month —just as soon as ever you can.'

Cathie raised startled eyes. Like someone sleep-walking, she put her hands before her. Alec caught both her hands in one of his own and with the other encircled her waist, pulling her against him.

'I love you, Cathie,' he said. Before she could answer, he bent his tall head and began to kiss her as if he would never let her go.

Cathie stood quite still in the tight circle of Alec's arm and something within her cried silently, 'No, no!'

Something within her belonged finally, unchangingly and for ever to Keith. She struggled free.

Alec let her go immediately. 'What's wrong, Cathie? Have I offended you?'

'No, no, of course not.'

Because hadn't she encouraged Alec all the evening? Hadn't she been striving desperately to put him in Keith's place? Alec was in love with her. Therefore she was to be in love with Alec so that she would forget Keith, so that the aching wound of separation would be healed.

Impossible. Alec was good, he was handsome and charming and kind, but Keith was part of herself. She loved him irretrievably, and Alec's kiss had shown her that she couldn't alter overnight.

Alec said again, 'Cathie.'

She turned, conscious that her eyes were filling with tears.

'It's all right, Alec. It's not your fault.'

Alec caught her hand. 'I've rushed you, Cathie. I didn't mean to, but I love you so much and you've been so very sweet to me all evening. I thought——'

Cathie shook her head. 'It's no good, Alec. I've tried. I've wanted to fall in love with you, but I can't.' She steadied her voice again. 'I'm sorry, I haven't been very fair to you.'

His fingers tightened on her own.

'Nonsense. I'm to blame—going at things like a bull in a china shop. I should have realised it's too soon yet. I don't want you just on the rebound, Cathie darling, but I'm not giving up hope. I know in time——'

'No, Alec,' Cathie broke in. 'No—I know that now.'

Since you kissed me, she thought. Funny that a kiss can be the beginning of something or the ending.

'I'm not giving up hope,' Alec repeated obstinately. He said in a lighter tone of voice, 'Come on, we'll finish the dance.'

They returned to the gaily decorated restaurant, just in time to hear the dance band end their music on a long rattle of drums and strike up immediately with 'God Save the Queen.'

'Why, it's the end,' Alec protested. 'Gosh, where's the evening got to?'

Cathie was silent, she was thankful it was over. She couldn't have borne the anti-climax of dancing with Alec, of trying to be as gay and animated as she had been earlier on. Everything seemed suddenly empty and futile now that she had come face to face with the truth and seen how false had been her hopes, how impossible it was to substitute Alec for Keith.

Sheila was standing near the cloakroom as if she were waiting for someone. She smiled at Cathie.

'Hasn't it been a super evening? I have enjoyed it,' she added. 'You look marvellous, Cathie. I love your dress.'

Kind Sheila. Brave, generous-hearted little Sheila!

Cathie said gently, 'Thank you. I've admired your red one all evening. Alec said you remind him of one of those dark red roses, a Crimson Glory or an Etoile de Hollande.'

'How nice of him.' Sheila looked over her shoulder. 'I'm waiting for Ann Haslam. She and her brother are giving me a lift home. Geoff had to leave earlier so as to catch his bus.'

'You go our way,' Cathie said impulsively. 'Isn't Langham Avenue off the Barnside Road? Alec and I can take you home.'

Sheila stared at her with frank brown eyes. 'No, thank you, Cathie. I'd rather not.'

Cathie laid her hand on Sheila's arm. 'Please, Sheila. Please do.'

Sheila met her look for a moment. She shrugged.

'All right. But three's a crowd, you know.' She turned to say something to a tall girl who came up behind her as Cathie went to find her coat.

'I've told Ann,' she said briefly when Cathie returned. 'It does save them quite a detour.'

Alec was waiting for them at the entrance. 'The car is round the side,' he said. He looked at Sheila in surprise.

'Please, Alec, I've told Sheila we can drop her at Langham Avenue. We pass it on the way out to Barnside,' Cathie interposed quickly.

'Of course,' Alec said courteously. He smiled at Sheila in a friendly fashion. 'Always room for one more.'

'Thank you, Alec.'

The three of them turned out of the narrow passageway, leading from the side entrance to Stirling's, which had been kept specially opened that night for the dance. The lights of a car shone a little way ahead against the kerb.

'This is us,' said Alec.

Someone stepped forward from the shadow of the store window—a tall figure with a gleam of white shirt front against a dark overcoat, hanging open. A deep voice said, 'Cathie.'

Cathie whirled round. The moon, cresting the layers of cloud, shone down with revealing clarity upon her startled face. 'Keith!'

They stood quite still, staring at one another across the space of street between them. The night wind blew Cathie's dark hair across her face and ruffled the sweeping folds of chiffon about her feet. Another couple went past them, their laughing voices echoing on the quiet air.

As if without movement the distance was bridged between them. Irresistibly, they were in one another's arms.

'My own dearest Cathie!'

'Keith!'

They held each other tight as if neither would ever let the other go.

'Cathie, I couldn't bear it over at the dance. It was like a nightmare. All those people—

Mother and Melanie and all her friends. All I could think about was you, my dear, dear Cathie. I had to come and tell you—I could never stop loving you.'

Cathie lifted her face from the broad, black-clad shoulder she had been pressed against.

'I could never stop loving you, Keith.'

She lifted a finger to trace the line of his cheek. They gazed at one another in silence. Alec and Sheila had ceased to exist for either of them.

Keith bent his head and kissed Cathie.

Love is a coming home. It is passion with sweetness, affection with ecstasy. It is friendship and warmth and rapture and delight. It comes once in a lifetime in its fullest perfection. One falls in love twice, thrice. One loves wholly and unreservedly only once.

Cathie couldn't have put into words her racing thoughts and emotions. She clung to Keith, sensing in the depth of her being the essence of such things. She only knew that somehow they had both been tested and had come together closer than ever because of that testing.

She said, 'It was my fault, darling. I should have had more faith.'

'No, it was mine,' Keith told her. 'I didn't understand. I didn't realise what was happening, how things must have seemed to you.' His arms tightened about her. 'But we couldn't quarrel, sweetheart. We couldn't let other people and circumstances separate us. What we have between us is something so wonderful and tremendous it's worth all the fight to hang on to it.'

Tears glittered in Cathie's eyes. 'I know.'

She caught her breath abruptly and pulling away from Keith, glanced over her shoulder. 'Alec,' she began. 'Alec's waiting in the car—and Sheila.'

Keith kept one arm about her. 'Come on,' he said. 'I'll explain—that I have to talk to you and that I'm taking you home.'

But Alec forestalled him. He was standing by the car door. He said abruptly, 'Hallo, Chandler.' In the moonlight, Cathie could see the smile turned on her—a smile that was gentle, wry and understanding, all in one.

'It's all right, Cathie, I understand. It never would have worked out, I see that now.' His voice altered. 'I'm taking Sheila home. I think we can squeeze in somebody's taxi if we hurry.' He turned back to Keith. 'If you want to use my car to take Cathie back to Barnside, you can have it.'

He pulled open the car door and helped Sheila down from where she had been sitting, out of the cold wind. The four of them stood on the frosty pavement for a silent moment, facing one another.

Keith held out his hand. 'Thank you, Hamilton—for everything.'

Cathie felt his own hand enfolded in Alec's long fingers. She said unsteadily, 'Goodnight, Alec. You've been terribly kind.' She met Sheila's warmly sympathetic gaze. 'Goodnight, Sheila.'

'Goodnight, Cathie.'

CHAPTER 12

KEITH drove a little way along the road in Alec's car, then he braked to a standstill in a narrow sidestreet.

He turned to Cathie and his arms closed about her as he drew her against his shoulder.

'Hamilton's been very decent.' He paused. 'He's in love with you, Cathie.'

'Yes. He—asked me to marry him,' Cathie said. 'Tonight at the dance. Oh, Keith, it was only then I realised how utterly hopeless it was— to try to get over you, I mean. I just couldn't. We're so much a part of each other.'

'I know,' Keith said.

Cathie raised her head and they kissed one another in the darkness. She sighed.

'And we've still a long way to go, Keith darling. Three more months before your exam.'

Keith's voice was firm and decided.

'I mean to get one or two matters settled. But tonight we're together again. That's all that matters.'

In a little while they drove on, Keith's hand reaching to clasp Cathie's from time to time as they drove along the road. It seemed no time at all before they were pulling to a standstill outside Dr. Nesbit's house. Keith got out and helped Cathie down. Brilliant moonlight sparkled on the frosted rooftop and turned the church spire into a silvered cone.

'I'll come out to see you tomorrow,' he said in the still quiet that encompassed them. 'Will that be all right?'

'Uncle Robert's coming home in the morning,' Cathie said doubtfully. 'I ought to stay and help. I have the morning off from the store. I expect Aunt Jean will be awfully busy.'

'Don't worry,' said Keith. He lifted her chin up with one finger. 'Would it be easier to meet me in Barrington about tea time?'

Cathie nodded. 'I think it would. It would be easier for Aunt Jean.'

'I'll meet the three-thirty train. Goodnight, my dearest. You know I shall love you for always.'

They held each other in a warm, loving embrace. Then Cathie put her key in the door and Keith stepped backwards towards the car. She stood waving until he was out of sight. She crept quietly up the stairs, tired but wonderfully happy. It had been a strange evening, but nothing mattered any more because Keith filled her world again.

In the morning, the house was in a turmoil. Aunt Jean was so excited and happy and on edge that she could not sit still for a minute and kept repeating her instructions over and over again.

'The ambulance will be here at eleven.' She glanced accusingly at Peter Lang across the breakfast table. 'You're sure now, you'll be back from your rounds? You'll not let anybody hold you up?'

Peter looked up from his fried sausages. He had a preoccupied air this morning as if he were pondering on some problem. 'No, of course not, Mrs. Nesbit.' He smiled fleetingly. 'I promised you.'

Aunt Jean shot up abruptly, like a jack-in-the-box.

'Did I leave the study window open enough?' she demanded of them and of herself. 'The fire's lit for warmth, but we want plenty of fresh air.'

'I'll go,' Cathie cried, pushing back her chair.

'No, I'll go myself. I want a word with Mrs. Crackan at the same time.'

Aunt Jean went bustling off. Cathie and Peter smiled at one another. They both said together, 'Did you enjoy the dance?'

Cathie answered first. 'Terrifically.' She thought of the wonderful ending to the evening. 'It was—perfect. Did you?'

'No—well, yes, I mean.'

Cathie raised an eyebrow. 'You don't seem very sure.'

Peter frowned. 'It was a thoroughly enjoyable evening.' He got up so abruptly from the breakfast table that the crockery rattled protestingly. He went over to the fireplace and began quickly filling his pipe. 'Do you mind?' he added, waving it at Cathie.

Cathie watched him in surprise. 'No, of course not. Please do.' She said, 'Weren't you very late home? I was back about one o'clock and you must have been after me.'

'Mr. Seymour very kindly invited us to his home for a drink and a sandwich after the dance.' Peter stared down at the crackling fire with his unlit pipe in his hand. 'Melanie Seymour is quite unlike anybody I've ever met.' He seemed to be talking to himself. 'Beautiful—yet human. A sort of goddess of plenty.' He became aware of Cathie, sitting silently at the breakfast table. 'I must be off to surgery, and then the rounds or I'll be breaking my promise to Mrs. Nesbit,' he said abruptly, and was gone.

Cathie stared at the door, closed so suddenly upon his exit. Then she stood up and began to stack the breakfast things together. She thought helplessly, He's fallen in love with Melanie. Oh dear!

By the time eleven o'clock came, Peter was

back, waiting to receive Dr. Nesbit, and Mrs.
Nesbit and Cathie, quite exhausted from run-
ning up and down the stairs on countless errands,
were waiting with him.

At last the ambulance swung over the narrow
bridge and drew smoothly to a standstill outside
the low stone house. Dr. Nesbit was lifted down
on a stretcher and carried into the study bedroom prepared for him.

He looked very thin and white and was
obviously tired by the journey. Peter saw him
settled in and Mrs. Nesbit sat with him until he
fell into a quiet sleep.

Lunch was a simple meal and Cathie carried
a fish soufflé in to the doctor, who had wakened
up. He looked a shadow of his big, burly self,
but his eyes twinkled into a familiar smile as he
saw Cathie.

'Well, lassie, this is the best medicine they
could prescribe for me now—to let me be home
again. Your aunt's made me a comfy bedroom.'

Cathie fixed the tray so that it stood securely
on its four legs across his knees. She bent and
kissed his cheek. 'There, Uncle Robert. You'll
feel better after you've eaten this.'

Dr. Nesbit grimaced. He looked like an elderly
baby, turning distastefully from its bottle. 'I'm
not so hungry,' he said.

'Aunt Jean says you're to try to eat it all,'

Cathie urged. 'She'll only worry if you don't.'

'Oh, I never cared for fish,' the doctor said, lifting up a fork with one hand and revealing a gaunt, bony wrist sticking out from the flannel pyjama sleeve. 'But I suppose I must do my best to please you.'

'There's a darling!'

He put the fork down again. 'Young Lang, now. He's settled down pretty well, I reckon. Your aunt seems to have taken a particular fancy to him. What's your opinion?'

'Eat your fish and don't talk,' Cathie said sternly. 'I'm not going to stay and let you chatter.' She turned away, but the doctor called her back.

'Very well. Very well. But it's still uncommon hot.' He looked at her from under his bushy eyebrows. 'He said he'd like to stay on with me. I'm thinking of taking him into partnership.' He added humbly, 'I only wanted you to help a sick old man with your good advice.'

'Uncle Robbie, you're an old fraud!' Cathie laughed. 'I think it would be a perfect arrangement, but my opinion won't make a scrap of difference either way if you've made your mind up. Now eat your fish.'

The house slid into a tranquil Saturday afternoon coma. Lunch was cleared away. Peter Lang went off into the surgery to work among his papers. Mrs. Nesbit took her knitting and sat quietly in the patch of sunlight at the foot of her husband's bed, while he slept the light, frequent sleep of convalescence.

Cathie washed and changed, tiptoed a good-bye round the door of the study bedroom and hurried away to the little station at the bottom of the slope.

Keith was waiting for her and it was like all the other times to go forward and meet his kiss and quick embrace, only somehow sweeter and more treasured because of all that had happened between them.

He tucked her hand in his arm and lead the way out of the echoing noise of the station. 'We'll get a bus here,' he said.

'Where are we going?' Cathie asked. She dimpled. 'I thought I might be asked to have some tea somewhere.'

'You'll be having tea,' Keith answered. 'I said I was bringing someone back to tea.'

Cathie glanced curiously at him. 'But where are we going?' she repeated.

'You'll see.'

A green and white bus lumbered to a stand-still in front of them. Keith's hand was firm under her elbow. 'Hop on!'

Cathie moved up to a seat at the front.

'Mystery drive,' she said. She pressed her

hand over his own. 'Darling, I'm so happy again.'

Keith turned his head. His eyes, deep and dark and loving, met her own. 'My blessed, so am I.'

Cathie stared through the window at the passing road. She said slowly, 'Keith, it's the Lorimore bus—it's the bus you catch to go home.'

Keith nodded. 'Correct. We're going home to tea.'

'Home to tea?' Cathie echoed. She looked at him doubtfully. 'You mean, to your home?' She hesitated. 'Is your mother expecting me?'

'I said I was bringing a guest back to tea. Don't look so worried, sweetheart—it's all right. I'm sure it's going to be all right.' He ducked his tall head to glance through the window. 'We're nearly there.'

They walked across the road in silence and turned the corner to Beechwood Crescent. She glanced sideways at Keith. 'Is—is it just us?' she asked.

He met her look, squeezed her arm tight against his side. 'Just us,' he answered. 'Melanie will not be there.'

'I didn't mean that——' Cathie began.

'I know you didn't, darling. I was only teasing.' His voice sobered again, 'Remember,

I love you with all my heart, Cathie. Nothing and no one will ever change that.'

He pushed open an iron gate before Cathie had time to reply and opened the cream-painted front door, standing aside for Cathie to enter.

For a moment she stood irresolute in the light, square, cream-washed hall. The drawing room door slowly opened. Mrs. Chandler's voice called softly, 'Is that you, Keith?'

She came forward into the hall and stopped dead, staring at Cathie in surprise.

Keith put his arm about Cathie's shoulders. 'I told you I was bringing a guest home to tea, Mother,' he said, and Cathie's heart jumped, for he couldn't hide the appeal in his voice.

Mrs. Chandler recovered herself.

'Of course. How very nice to see you, Catherine. Please come in here.' She led the way into the charmingly furnished room that Cathie remembered so well.

She gestured gracefully towards an armchair. 'Do sit down. You must forgive my surprise. To tell you the truth, I was really expecting to see someone else.' She glanced down at Cathie's silent face and then at Keith. She added challengingly, 'I was really expecting to see Melanie. She is in and out of here so often with Keith.'

Cathie could see Keith's jaw tighten. This wasn't going the way he wanted it. His mother's enmity was not to be overcome.

'I'd like you to explain to Cathie, Mother, that Melanie is in and out of here, as you put it, at your invitation, not mine.'

His mother stared at him. Her smooth face was set into rigid lines. She sat down rather abruptly in the chair just behind her. Her thin fingers clasped one another on the silken lap of her dress.

'What a peculiar remark to make, Keith! I can't think how it can possibly concern Catherine who invites anyone here.'

Keith stood very tall and upright in front of the glowing, log fire.

'It does, Mother. All along you've been at great pains to make Cathie feel that I'm involved in some way with Melanie, and I'd like you to explain to her that it's quite otherwise.'

Cathie made a move forward in her chair. She felt suddenly uncomfortable for Mrs. Chandler. 'Keith, please!'

Keith held up a hand.

'No, Cathie, I'm sorry. I brought you here tonight, thinking that Mother would see that we love each other and nothing will change it.'

Mrs. Chandler's usually pale face was almost deathlike in its pallor. Her slender hands clasped and unclasped themselves unceasingly. She turned her head slowly to stare at Cathie. 'Are you responsible for this?' she bit out in a low voice.

Keith moved forward.

'Of course Cathie's not responsible. If you want to know the truth Cathie gave me up rather than go against your wishes, but I wouldn't let her. I wouldn't let her wreck our two lives.' His voice softened. 'I'm sorry, Mother. I just want you to accept the fact that we love each other and that nothing will change us.'

'And if I don't?' Mrs. Chandler said slowly.

'If you don't, Mother, then I'll chuck up my law studies and get a job—any job—and marry Cathie the very first day I can do so. I wanted to do that before, but Cathie wouldn't let me. She said it wouldn't be fair to you.' He laughed with an edge of bitterness. 'I wonder just how fair you've been to Cathie!'

Mrs. Chandler had risen to her feet. Her still face was suddenly working.

CHAPTER 13

For a moment, Mrs, Chandler stood there sway-
ing uncertainly. Keith moved forward. 'Are you
all right, Mother?'

The burning dark eyes held his gaze, then
closed slowly, as if shutting out some unwanted
sight. Mrs. Chandler pressed the back of her hand
against her forehead.

Keith put his hand under her arm. 'Sit down,
Mother.' His voice was firm and kind. 'I'm
afraid this has been rather a shock to you.'

Mrs. Chandler shook his hand away. 'I can't
discuss it with you. I feel too ill.' She turned
slowly towards the door. 'I'm going upstairs to
lie down.' She stared at Cathie as if she were a
piece of furniture obstructing her way.

Cathie made a helpless gesture. She wanted to
say something—to apologise, but for what? Was
she sorry because Keith had taken so firm a
stand?

'I'll help you upstairs, Mother,' Keith began.
'I—didn't mean to distress you.'

Mrs. Chandler raised a thin hand in protest. 'A
slight feeling of faintness.' Her voice was coldly

ironic. 'I want only to be left alone.'

She turned to the bend of the stairs and went up, slim and stiffly upright.

Cathie and Keith watched her out of sight. Then Keith moved back into the drawing-room. His dark eyes were rueful as they met hers. 'I don't seem to have done a lot of good, do I?'

'You couldn't help it, Keith. I hope we haven't —I hope she isn't really ill.'

'It's just the shock of things,' he said. 'But I wish she'd really been able to talk it over with us, instead of going off like that in the middle of things.'

Cathie was silent. There were moments when she felt she knew Mrs. Chandler much better than her son did. Escape was typical of her. To stay and fight things out was something she would never do.

'Anyway,' Keith went on, 'she knows how I feel about everything now. She knows that I'm going to marry you and that I've seen right through all this Melanie Seymour nonsense.' He stared down at Cathie, smiled suddenly. 'Rather an anti-climax, isn't it? I saw us all feasting on the fatted calf. Now I feel we ought to clear out, go down town somewhere.'

'I feel that too,' Cathie told him. The still house, silent save for the ticking of the gilt clock on the mantelpiece and the soft hiss of the fire, oppressed her. 'We could go to a cinema.'

'Just the thing,' Keith agreed, then he paused and listened.

Cathie understood him. 'Go up and see if there's anything we can do. Perhaps—we could make some tea or something.'

Keith nodded. 'I'd better just inquire.' He went quickly up the stairs. Cathie heard him knock on a door, heard a muffled exchange of words. He came down again, almost immediately.

'The door's locked. I think she's lying down. She doesn't want anything,' he added. 'She says if she wants any tea, she'll get it for herself later.' He lifted Cathie's coat up from the chest in the hall. 'Come on, sweetheart. I'm afraid there's nothing for it but the Connaught.'

Cathie smiled up at him as he put the coat and his arms about her. 'We've practically bought the Connaught with our custom!'

Out in the street they both felt lighthearted again.

'What will your mother do now?' Cathie asked.

'Oh, she'll come round—I mean, she's just got to.' His firm brown chin tilted aggressively.

Cathie laid a gentle hand on his arm.

'I don't want you to hurt your mother, Keith. I wish she had come round.' She added wistfully, 'I can't think what our next meeting is going to be like.'

'Don't worry, darling. It will all work out.'

Nevertheless, she worried during the rest of the weekend. If Mrs. Chandler was not going to make some gesture of reconciliation, it meant that there was nothing ahead but a break between her and Keith.

All Sunday morning she waited on tenterhooks, thinking the telephone would ring, that Keith would be there to issue an invitation from his mother for that afternoon or that evening. Or it would be Mrs. Chandler herself speaking.

The afternoon came and with it Keith, as arranged, out to Barnside for tea and supper. Cathie met him anxiously at the door. 'Hallo, darling.'

'Hallo, sweet.' He pulled her close against him and kissed her.

'How—how is your mother?' Cathie managed to say at last.

He frowned. 'She's been in bed all morning— said she had a bad headache. She didn't sleep very well, I gather.'

'Have you left her on her own?' Cathie asked. She felt suddenly conscience-stricken. 'I mean, is she still in bed? Is there no one to look after her?'

'Doris will be in later,' he said briefly. 'But Mother said she was going out to tea or something.' He glanced down at Cathie. 'Darling, you're worrying. What's the matter? Is it Mother? She'll come round all right. We'll just have to give her time.'

'Yes, of course.'

Cathie led him through into the sitting-room, where Peter Lang sat on one side of the fire. He jumped up immediately when he saw Keith.

'Oh, hallo.' They shook hands warmly. Aunt Jean came in, beaming a welcome, then took Keith off on his own to see Dr. Nesbit while Cathie went out into the kitchen to finish preparing the tea things.

It was Sunday, like so many other past Sundays—homely, happy, comfortable. But an undercurrent of disquiet ran through it all for Cathie and she couldn't rest. It seemed as if Keith had brought matters to a head and yet the issue was still unsettled. Mrs. Chandler had refused to face things there and then, but that she would act eventually, Cathie was sure. But what would she do?

'It's only two weeks to Christmas,' Aunt Jean observed. 'Gracious, how the year's flown! It will be New Year before we know and a fresh beginning.'

'A year ago, I was in hospital for Christmas and New Year,' Peter Lang said. 'I was still on a diet, so all the good things passed me by.' He smiled. 'I shall make up for it this year!'

Cathie was silent. Last year her father had been alive and they had all been together at Willowmere. Keith had come up to dinner on New Year's Eve. Other young people had been there. There had been dancing. One short year ago—a lifetime.

Keith's fingers closed over hers under cover of the tablecloth.

'Never mind last year,' he said lightly. 'What about next year? We'll be married by then, won't we, Cathie?'

She smiled rather wistfully. 'I hope so, darling.'

Aunt Jean gave her a quick look.

'Of course you will be.' She turned to Peter Lang. 'Then it will be the doctor's turn.'

Peter shook his head. 'I'm afraid not. The—sort of girl I aspire to wouldn't look at me.'

Aunt Jean raised a questioning eyebrow. 'That looks as if you have someone in view.'

His pale face flushed into sudden colour. 'No, no, of course not. I only meant—if I had—well, I'm—I'm only doing locum work. I'm not even in practice yet.'

Aunt Jean smiled mysteriously. 'Oh, I'm sure that will be remedied soon, so you'll be able to up and ask her.' She saw Peter's embarrassed glance and tapped his arm with a plump hand. 'It's only my teasing. You mustn't mind me.'

The signs of Christmas and New Year were gaily manifest at Stirling's the next morning when Cathie went back to work.

Meeting Alec again wasn't going to be easy. Working under him was going to be more difficult still. Cathie felt a pang as she hurried along the narrow passage between the studio and the advertising offices.

Molly Fanshawe was already there. She gestured a casual salute in Cathie's direction and went on unwrapping the parcel on her desk.

Cathie took her coat and hat off and turned to the mirror. Molly said from behind her, 'Isn't he angelic?' She held aloft an enormous black and white panda. 'It's for Trudy. One of her presents.'

'Oh, gorgeous,' said Cathie. She smiled. 'I've only just become aware of it all—Christmas, I mean. I can see I'll have to make up for lost time if I hope to catch up with my shopping.'

'I can't think how you overlooked it,' Molly remarked dryly. 'Seeing that Stirling's start getting steamed up about it some time around the last week in August.' She laughed. 'Well, all but. I haven't seen you since the dance, have I? Did you have fun? Oh, of course, you went with Alec, didn't you? So you'll have heard the news.'

'What news?' asked Cathie. She sat down at

her desk and pulled open the centre drawer.

"About Alec's transfer. I'd no idea he was putting in for a move, but I expect he mentioned it to you. You're both so pally.'

Cathie sat arrested with a sheaf of drawings in one hand. She said slowly, 'No, Alec didn't say anything. Do you mean—do you mean he's leaving Stirling's?'

Molly tenderly packed tissue paper round the panda's furry body.

'He's gone. He saw Mr. Wales on Saturday morning and I understand he went up to Edinburgh over the weekend.'

Alec gone! Advertising without Alec, without his friendly warmth and gaiety and laughter. It would never be quite the same without him. She would miss him, but perhaps it was for the best this way. Only——

She said, 'He's gone to another job.'

Molly nodded, laying the parcel in a corner behind her.

'Of course. He's gone to the Stirling's branch there. I expect he'll end up Advertising Manager. It's probably a promotion.'

'I hope so,' said Cathie. 'If anyone deserves it, it's Alec.'

Molly was looking curiously at her. 'Odd, he never spoke about it to you. I mean—so soon before it happened.' She broke off abruptly. 'Oh well, it was probably all confidential or something. You know how these things are.' She smiled at Cathie. 'I don't know who's coming in his place, but I hope he's got half Alec's sense of humour. I say, look at this extraordinary scarf I've bought. It has a printed head of every British pop star. My young cousin is going to adore it. She's at that phase.'

'It's most amusing,' Cathie said in reply. She was thinking that Alec had gone because of her. She had been the reason for his transfer.

It seemed strange to be working directly under Mr. Wales. The series of bookmarkers were finished. The next job on hand was the January sales catalogue—a bulky affair, amply illustrated and photographed.

Sheila was at her accustomed place in the canteen when lunch time came.

'Hallo, Cathie,' she smiled rather shyly— Sheila, who was usually so open and friendly and forthcoming. She said quickly, 'The toad-in-the-hole is nice today. I've just had some.' She glanced at Cathie and hesitated. Then she said in a little rush of words, 'I'm so glad everything's turned out all right for you—with Keith.' She paused and added, looking away from Cathie, 'I expect you've heard Alec's gone.'

'Yes, Molly told me.'

'We shall miss him terrifically.' Sheila's brown eyes met Cathie's. 'Alec asked me to write to him —just to give him the news, to keep in touch sort of thing.'

'I'm glad,' Cathie smiled.

'Yes.' It was a sigh rather than a word. Then Sheila said matter-of-factly, 'How is your uncle?'

'He's heaps better. He came home from the hospital on Saturday.'

'Oh good, that's great news.'

Words masked so much a feeling of regret. If she, Cathie, hadn't come to Stirling's, perhaps Alec would have stayed on, perhaps he would have fallen in love with Sheila, but life was always moving onward, the page was always being turned.

It was closing time. Cathie walked slowly out of the side entrance, making a mental list of Christmas presents to be bought. She stared in through the big plate-glass window as she went past—washing machines and spin-dryers, wheel-barrows and electric irons—not very inspiring. The next window was books and stationery, some nice notepaper. Notepaper—quite a good suggestion for someone who wrote a lot of letters. She smiled rather sadly—for Sheila to write to Alec on.

A hand caught her arm. 'Hallo!'

It was Keith. Cathie stared at him in surprise.

'Hallo, darling. I wasn't expecting to see you here.'

'I've got some news for you,' Keith said. His voice sounded warm and excited. He turned his head. 'Melanie's here too.'

Cathie's stare of surprise deepened as she saw the tall figure of Melanie Seymour appear from behind Keith. She was wearing her fur coat with a fur hat on her blonde hair. She smiled at Cathie—a slow, sweet smile that was so much a part of her. 'Hallo, Cathie.'

The two tall figures stood side by side, smiling at Cathie until she felt she was dreaming.

'We had to come and tell you together,' Melanie said in her deep voice. 'It's so absolutely amazing. I couldn't let Keith shatter you with it on your own.'

Cathie felt rather stupid. She said, 'But what is it? What's happened?'

'Tell her, Melanie,' Keith urged.

'No, you tell her.' Melanie slid her arm through Keith's. 'Tell her that you and I are members of the same family now.' She laughed. 'It's really the most fantastic notion!'

Keith met Cathie's puzzled stare. He said abruptly, 'Mother's gone to London—to be married to Melanie's father.'

'Married? To Mr. Seymour?'

Keith and Melanie nodded simultaneously.

'Yes,' said Keith. 'Isn't it astonishing?'

'I do think Papa's an old dark horse,' said Melanie. 'I'd just no idea he had this project up his sleeve.' She glanced sideways at Keith out of glorious blue eyes. 'I thought they were match-making for us.'

Keith laughed without embarrassment. Without obvious effort, he freed himself from Melanie and reached Cathie's hand.

'Darling, this is only the start of the news. Wait until you hear the rest. Mother left a letter for me.' He fumbled with his other hand in his breast pocket. 'Here we are. Read it, Cathie.'

CHAPTER 14

Cathie unfolded the sheet of paper in her hand, while Keith and Melanie stood by in silence to watch her read it.

'My dear Keith, [Mrs. Chandler wrote]

'I expect this will be a great surprise to you, but by the time you receive this letter, Harold Seymour and I will be on our way to London to be married. We have been long and close friends for many years, as you know, even during your father's lifetime, but I had never chosen to see in his deep regard for me anything more than a sharing of our mutual ambitions. You know very well what those were. I have never sought personal happiness. I have only tried to live for you. You showed me how useless and unnecessary this was on Saturday. You showed me all too clearly that you were bent on living your own life.

'I do not expect to return to Barrington for some months as Harold is going to South America on a business trip shortly before Christmas and I am accompanying him. I am making arrangements for the house to be closed up and I suggest you find comfortable rooms somewhere.

'As my financial position in the future is likely to be greatly altered, I am now prepared to settle upon you some of the income left in trust to me by your father. This means you will have a certain amount of independence in the future and will be able to pursue your headstrong plans to your heart's content.

'I will send you a forwarding address later. I am afraid I cannot write as warmly and affectionately as I should do in other circumstances. Your conduct on Saturday was a great shock to me. Nevertheless, I remain,

Your loving mother,
Gertrude Chandler.'

Cathie read the letter slowly, re-reading some of the phrases a second time. It was a bitter letter for all its gestures, but reading between the lines she could see that Mrs. Chandler had left the door open, that she would return when time had softened the blow to forgive Keith and be reconciled with him.

She glanced up at him as she held the letter out.

'I'm sorry,' she said inadequately, 'That it's happened like this. Do you mind very much!'

'No,' Keith answered surprisingly. 'I think it's all worked out for the best. Mother ought to have married again long ago instead of concentrating on me. She'd have been much happier.' He looked round at Melanie. 'She and your old man were made for each other. She'll adore all that entertaining—all the high life.' He squeezed Cathie's hand. 'And you realize what it means for us—that we can be married just as soon as possible. Oh, gosh, darling, you'll never know how hopeless I've felt about things at times!'

Cathie smiled rather shakily. 'Or me.'

'Hey,' Melanie put in, 'I'm still here!'

Cathie turned to her. 'What will you do, Melanie, while your father's away? Will you stay on at your house alone?'

Melanie shrugged.

'The house runs itself. We have a marvellous housekeeper.' She turned to Keith. 'But I'm going to feel very lonely now you've gone and got all tied up.'

'And I'm going to feel responsible for you, darn it,' Keith grinned, 'now that I'm your half-brother. What shall we do with her?'

Cathie smiled at Melanie. 'I know someone else at Barnside who could do with some cheering up. What about taking Melanie back with us?'

'Splendid,' said Keith. He caught hold of an arm of each. 'Come on, Melanie. Let's go and find your car.'

As they crossed the space of car park Melanie

turned to glance sideways at Cathie. Her blue gaze was suddenly serious. She said slowly, 'I do wish you every happiness, Cathie. You deserve it—both of you. You've both fought and won. You see, Mrs. Chandler wasn't the only one who had hopes for Keith and myself. I had them once too, but Keith didn't have to tell me as he had to tell his mother that he would never give you up. I learnt to see that for myself quite early on.' She held out a sudden hand. 'I hope we're going to be friends, Cathie.'

Cathie put her own out. She said steadily, 'I know we are, Melanie.'

Because you're generous, she thought. Generous in mind and heart. She thought again of Peter Lang. This girl so utterly different, so opposite in every way, would yet be good for him. She had an instinctive knowledge of that. She thought wryly, I'm worse than Mrs. Chandler—matchmaking!

'Are you sure it's all right, my coming back with you?' Melanie asked as they drove along the road to Barnside. 'Won't your aunt be surprised?'

'She'll be delighted, I assure you,' Cathie said with a smile.

The lights of the house shone ahead, out on to the cobbled street. 'Here we are,' Cathie said as Melanie brought the car to a standstill. She slid out and ran up the three steps to the front door. Just as she put her hand on the knob it opened inwards and Peter Lang stood there.

'I've brought a visitor,' Cathie told him. She stepped aside so that Peter, looking down, saw Melanie Seymour's beautiful, smiling face, framed against the dark street as she gazed up at him.

For a moment he seemed too stunned to speak. Melanie broke the pause.

'I'm always turning up here, aren't I? Like a bad penny.' She held out her hand. 'I hope you're pleased to see me.'

Peter swallowed. 'I can't tell you how pleased. I say, do come in.'

Keith caught hold of Cathie's hand.

'Let them go. I want to have you to myself for moment or two.' His arms enfolded her. 'Darling, isn't it wonderful that all our troubles are over? We can be married right away.'

Cathie rubbed her cheek softly against his. Over his shoulder she saw the thin crescent of a new moon. She sighed with a deep and overwhelming happiness. She pulled Keith round to face the other way.

'You wish too,' she said. Keith cocked an eyebrow up at the silver curve above him.

'I've nothing left to wish for,' he said, and bent his head to kiss her.

Poignant tales of love, conflict, romance and adventure

Harlequin Presents...

Elegant and sophisticated novels of **great romantic fiction . . .**
12 All time best sellers.

Join the millions of avid Harlequin readers all over the world who delight in the magic of a really exciting novel.

From the library of Harlequin Presents all time best sellers — we are proud and pleased to make available the 12 selections listed here.

Combining all the essential elements you expect of great story telling, and bringing together your very favourite authors — you'll thrill to these exciting tales of love, conflict, romance, sophistication and adventure. You become involved with characters who are interesting, vibrant, and alive. Their individual conflicts, struggles, needs, and desires, grip you, the reader, until the final page.

Have you missed any of these *Harlequin Presents...*

Offered to you in the sequence in which they were originally printed — this is an opportunity for you to add to your Harlequin Presents . . . library.

This elegant and sophisticated series was first introduced in 1973, and has been a huge success ever since. The world's top romantic fiction authors combine glamour, exotic locales, dramatic and poignant love themes woven into gripping and absorbing plots to create an unique reading experience in each novel.

You'd expect to pay $1.75 or more for this calibre of best selling novel, — at only **$1.25 each,** Harlequin Presents are truly top value, top quality entertainment.

Don't delay — order yours today

Complete and mail this coupon today!